THE WICKED WIDOW

Barbara Cartland

Barbara Cartland Ebooks Ltd

This edition © 2021

Copyright Cartland Promotions 1993

ISBNs

9781788675338   EPUB

9781788675345   PAPERBACK

Book design by M-Y Books
m-ybooks.co.uk

THE BARBARA CARTLAND ETERNAL COLLECTION

The Barbara Cartland Eternal Collection is the unique opportunity to collect all five hundred of the timeless beautiful romantic novels written by the world's most celebrated and enduring romantic author.

Named the Eternal Collection because Barbara's inspiring stories of pure love, just the same as love itself, the books will be published on the internet at the rate of four titles per month until all five hundred are available.

The Eternal Collection, classic pure romance available worldwide for all time .

THE LATE DAME BARBARA CARTLAND

Barbara Cartland, who sadly died in May 2000 at the grand age of ninety eight, remains one of the world's most famous romantic novelists. With worldwide sales of over one billion, her outstanding 723 books have been translated into thirty six different languages, to be enjoyed by readers of romance globally.

Writing her first book 'Jigsaw' at the age of 21, Barbara became an immediate bestseller. Building upon this initial success, she wrote continuously throughout her life, producing bestsellers for an astonishing 76 years. In addition to Barbara Cartland's legion of fans in the UK and across Europe, her books have always been immensely popular in the USA. In 1976 she achieved the unprecedented feat of having books at numbers 1 & 2 in the prestigious B. Dalton Bookseller bestsellers list.

Although she is often referred to as the 'Queen of Romance', Barbara Cartland also wrote several historical biographies, six autobiographies and numerous theatrical plays as well as books on life, love, health and cookery. Becoming one of Britain's most popular media personalities and dressed in her trademark pink, Barbara spoke on radio and television about social and political issues, as well as making many public appearances.

In 1991 she became a Dame of the Order of the British Empire for her contribution to literature and her work for humanitarian and charitable causes.

Known for her glamour, style, and vitality Barbara Cartland became a legend in her own lifetime. Best remembered for her wonderful romantic novels and loved by millions of readers worldwide, her books remain treasured for their heroic heroes, plucky heroines and traditional values. But above all, it was Barbara Cartland's overriding belief in the positive power of love to help, heal and improve the quality of life for everyone that made her truly unique.

AUTHOR'S NOTE

Many Castles in England have secret passages, one reason being that if the owner had a mistress, he could go to her without being seen.

Another was that at the time of King Henry VIII and the Dissolution of the Monasteries, the Monks could hide in them and not be slaughtered by the King's men.

It was because of Henry's desire to be free of a barren wife that he turned against the Roman Catholic Church, having been refused permission to divorce and remarry so that he could produce an heir.

This was a turning point in England as far as religion was concerned and resulted in the reigning Monarch becoming the Head of the Church of England.

The highwayman of the eighteenth century became a romantic figure in a great many novels.

Mounted usually on a fine horse, which could carry him away quickly from the scene of the crime, his dark clothes and his rakish appearance made him the 'Gentleman of the Road'.

There were, however, other highwaymen who were forced into obtaining enough money to live, simply because they had been so badly treated after the War with France was ended.

Men who had fought valiantly for their country came home to find that there were no jobs for them to do, their wives had often died or run away with another man or their cottages were inhabited by someone else. There were no pensions for them, not even for those who were wounded.

These men, like Bill in my story, were rough but not cruel nor were they in the same category as the romantic highwaymen written about by Alfred Noyes,

> *"And he rode with a jewelled twinkle.*
> *His pistol butts a-twinkle.*
> *His rapier hilt a-twinkle.*
> *Under the jewelled sky."*

CHAPTER ONE
1821

Standing in the shadows on the landing, Kyla heard the old butler shuffling over the hall to the front door.

She had been waiting for some time.

Now at last the bell had rung and he had come as raidly as he could from the pantry.

She knew that he could not move quickly because he had arthritis in his ankles.

He had hoped when her father died that he would be retired on a pension. He was in fact provided for in her father's will, but her stepmother had insisted that old Dawkins stay on.

It was not that she had any affection for him but she knew well that she would not find another butler as well up in his duties so cheaply.

Stumbling a little because the hall was only dimly lit, Dawkins opened the front door and let in a man.

"You have been a long time," he said in a disagreeable voice.

"I'm sorry, sir," Dawkins replied, "but it is quite a way from the pantry and I'm not as young as I used to be."

George Hunter, who Kyla knew was always rude to the servants, did not answer him.

He merely threw his hat down on a chair and walked without being announced into the sitting room.

He closed the door sharply behind him and, as Dawkins went back to the pantry, Kyla tiptoed down the stairs in her stockinged feet.

She crossed the hall without making a sound and, reaching the door of the sitting room, she bent down to listen intently at the keyhole.

Lady Shenley had also been waiting but much more comfortably in an armchair with a glass of brandy beside her.

When the door opened and George Hunter came in, she sprang to her feet with a cry.

"How could you have been so long?"

"I am sorry, Sybil," George Hunter replied, "but the man I wanted to see was in Court and then I had to take him out to dinner and fill him up with wine before he would tell me what I wanted to know."

"That is what I am waiting for, George," Sybil Shenley said, "and, of course, you."

She put her arms round his neck and he kissed her rather roughly.

Then, putting her aside, he went to the grog table in a corner of the room and poured himself out a large brandy.

Sybil Shenley was watching him closely.

It was obvious that she was impatient for him to come back to her side to tell her what she so wanted to know.

George Hunter, however, drank quite a lot of the brandy before he finally threw himself down in a chair.

It was on the other side of the fireplace and he stretched out his legs.

"I am *damned* tired, if you want to know," he said. "Hanging about a Law Court, where there is nowhere to sit, is not exactly a picnic."

"I was afraid you would be delayed," Sybil said. "But now you have seen this Counsel, who is supposed to be so clever. What did he say?"

George Hunter took another gulp of brandy and then he started slowly,

"He told me that there was no chance in Hell of your breaking the Will and, as long as there is a Lord Shenley in existence, the money is his for life."

He paused for a moment and then went on,

"In the event of his death, without leaving an heir, everything goes to the girl."

Sybil Shenley gave a cry of horror.

"Is that true? Is there really no way out?"

George Hunter shook his head.

"None at all, unless the boy dies and the girl is disposed of."

There was a long poignant silence.

The silence seemed almost to vibrate round and round the room.

Then Sybil Shenley muttered,

"I suppose, although it is unpleasant, that is what we shall have to do."

George Hunter sat up in his chair.

"What are you talking about, Sybil, or are you joking?"

"I am not joking," Sybil Shenley replied, "for I have no intention of being a pauper or living on the charity of my stepchildren."

"You are their legal Guardian until they reach the age of twenty-one, which, where Terry is concerned, will not be for many years."

"You have not read the Will as carefully as I have," Sybil Shenley snapped. "There are Trustees to interfere, all tiresome men whom my husband trusted. One of those, as you well know, is the Solicitor."

There was silence and then George Hunter asked,

"And what do you intend to do about it?"

"What you have already told me," Sybil Shenley said. "The boy will have an unfortunate accident and we can marry the girl off. What is the name of that Lord you told me about who has a passion for virgins?"

"He could not marry her," George Hunter pointed out. "He has a wife."

Sybil Shenley shrugged her shoulders.

"Then she can be his mistress."

"I should imagine that, seeing that Lord Frome is such a very unpleasant chap, she will refuse."

Sybil Shenley laughed.

"Really, George, you are so naïve. You don't suppose that I shall ask the girl's approval to marry her to anyone who I think is suitable?"

She paused and, as George Hunter did not speak, she carried on,

"You always underrate my intelligence. I know where Madam Bassett, who keeps that 'House of Pleasure' at the corner of Leicester Square, buys the drugs that she gives the girls when they first enter her establishment."

"How the hell did you find that out?" George Hunter asked in an amused voice.

"I patronise the chemist where she goes for a reason of my own," Sybil Shenley replied. "And while I was talking to him, Madam came in. She asked him for what she wanted in a whisper, but I am very sharp of hearing."

"I must admit, Sybil, that you never miss a trick," George Hunter declared.

"A nice mess we would both be in if I did," Sybil Shenley sneered.

She thought for a moment before she added,

"That tiresome girl, Kyla, will take enough of the drug to make her amenable and when she does not know if it is Christmas or Easter, you can take her to Lord Frome."

"It is certainly a good idea," George Hunter said, "and I will see to it that Frome pays up handsomely for the privilege."

"Of course" Sybil Shenley agreed, "and that leaves us with the boy."

"I am not doing anything," George Hunter stipulated firmly, "that could mean ending up on the gallows."

"Of course not," Sybil Shenley agreed. "You know, dearest, that I have no wish to lose you."

"Then just be very careful in what you are planning where the boy is concerned," George Hunter said sternly.

"Remember he is now Lord Shenley and people have a nasty habit of keeping their eyes on a young Lord even if he is only eight years old."

"That is exactly what makes it very much easier," Sybil Shenley explained. "Small boys climb up on roofs and it is very easy to slip over a parapet. They also swim in lakes or fall into them from leaky canoes. Really, George, you should learn to use your imagination."

"It is not as active as yours," George Hunter admitted, "and, quite frankly, you make me nervous."

He finished his brandy, rose from the chair and walked over to the table to refill his glass.

Then he stood in front of the fireplace. There was no fire, but it was filled with flowers because it was summer.

Slowly, as if he was thinking everything through, he said again,

"You are making me feel nervous and we must consider it all very carefully before we do anything."

He drew in his breath before he went on,

"Quite a number of people will think it damned strange if Terry has an accident and Kyla takes up a life of sin with that dissolute Frome."

"Really, George, you are being positively ridiculous," Sybil Shenley exclaimed. "You don't suppose I have not thought of that?"

She gave a haughty laugh before she went on,

"Of course you will have to suggest to Frome when you hand the girl over to him and God knows, she is very much more attractive than the Cyprians and milkmaids with whom he usually spends his time that he must take her to France or some other place where no one will ask questions."

"You are making it sound easy," George Hunter said in an irritated tone. "But Kyla has a will of her own as I learnt when she slapped my face."

"As I will slap it if I find you playing about with her again," Sybil Shenley said sharply.

"I was only giving her a fatherly kiss because she was unhappy about the death of the old man," George Hunter said defensively.

"There is nothing fatherly about you," Sybil Shenley retorted. "You keep your hands and your lips to yourself or rather for me. Otherwise I will not pay your debts and the duns will be after you."

"All right, all right," George Hunter said. "I have the message and I will do what you tell me about the girl. But I warn you, the boy is going to be much more difficult."

"Not if we are sensible, George," Sybil Shenley said. "We will go to the country at the end of the week and by that time I shall have decided whether I shall buy a horse, which is guaranteed to kick him off or whether, as I have already suggested, he explores the roof and accidentally falls off it."

She appeared to be thinking before she continued,

"Alternatively he can drown in the lake. There is no reason for you to be involved in any of that."

"Thank Heavens for small mercies," George Hunter said. "But, if you ask me, I think it is too soon. Let's wait for a month or two and see what we can sell in the meantime."

Sybil Shenley gave a shriek.

"Sell?" she said. "There is nothing worth selling that is not entailed to that tiresome little boy. I have gone through the inventory word by word. The only things that are exempt are not worth a five shilling piece."

"Are you sure of that?" George Hunter asked. "I was going to ask you tonight for some money."

"I remembered that," Sybil Shenley answered. "I have fifty pounds for you upstairs, but it may be difficult to get much more for a week or so."

George Hunter scratched the side of his face.

"Fifty quid is better than nothing," he sighed. "The tradesmen are being most unpleasant and so is my landlord for that matter. Why the hell cannot I move in here?"

"Because I don't want to be talked about," she explained. "You know as well as I do that the *Beau Ton* would be horrified at my taking a lover so soon after poor old Arthur's death."

She spoke in an affected tone and George Hunter laughed.

"Poor Arthur! He never had the slightest idea of what was going on under his very nose."

"I don't suppose that everyone else was quite so blind," Sybil Shenley warned him. "As I have told you, George, it is sensible for us to lie low and for me to be a mourning widow until it is possible for us to be married."

"I am damned if I am going to be barred from coming with you to the country," George insisted.

'That is different," Sybil Shenley said. "Of course you will come with me to Shenley House. I have asked two other people to make it a party."

"Who are they?" George Hunter demanded.

"The half-witted Lady Briggs, who is always fawning on me," Sybil Shenley replied, "and her husband, who is a bore but very respectable."

"Oh, my God!" George Hunter exclaimed. "Do we have to have them?"

"It is so essential that they should be there as eyewitnesses to the tragedy that will occur when small children have no sense and are quite incapable of looking after themselves."

"I see the point," George Hunter muttered.

"Of course, as we are both very devoted to dear little Terry, I shall cry on Lord Briggs's shoulder while you weep on Violet's."

"I shall have to be blind drunk to do that," he retorted.

"Well, there is plenty of good claret in the cellar," Sybil Shenley informed him.

"That, at least, is some consolation," George replied. "And talking of drink, let me fill up your glass."

"There is a bottle of champagne in the ice cooler" Sybil said. "I was only calming my nerves with brandy until I knew what you had found out."

"Which is damned all!" George growled.

He walked towards the table in the corner.

On reaching it he started to pour the champagne, which was open in the ice cooler, into two glasses.

"Now that problem is settled, George, dear," Sybil Shenley said in a cooing voice, "we can enjoy ourselves."

George Hunter handed her a glass of champagne.

"Let us hope this calms my nerves," he said, "but I have an uncomfortable feeling, Sybil, that you thrive on crime."

"That is a very unkind thing to say," Sybil complained, but she did not sound angry.

"I have been wondering," George replied, "if poor old Arthur really died a natural death. It certainly puzzled the doctors as to why he should pop off at sixty."

"Then let it puzzle you too," Sybil said. "All you have to concern yourself with is me and me and me! I love you, George. If I have ever done anything wrong, it is because I love you."

George drank down half his glass of champagne.

"I suppose that is the truth," he said. "All right, come here. Come here!"

He put out his left arm and Sybil Shenley moved close to him, lifting her red lips to his.

As he kissed her, Kyla, outside the door, straightened herself.

She had heard enough.

The sooner she was back in the safety of her bedroom the better.

She was, however, not so foolish as to hurry.

She now moved on tiptoe just in case by some mischance her stepmother and her lover should hear her.

She had been able to hear quite clearly everything that they had said.

Only as she crept upstairs did the horror of it sweep over her like a tidal wave.

How could anyone be so wicked, so cruel and so brutal?

How could her stepmother plan to kill her brother Terry and to force her into the arms of a ghastly old man, who she knew was a byword for debauchery?

She reached the top landing.

She was just going to her own room when she remembered that her stepmother had said that there was fifty pounds waiting for George Hunter upstairs.

She hesitated.

Then she told herself that if she was to save Terry and herself she had to have money.

Although she had been anticipating that something like this would happen, she did not have enough in her possession.

She slipped into her stepmother's room, knowing that there would be no maid on duty.

When the champagne was finished, they would both come up the stairs and drunkenly fall into bed. It was what they had done almost every night since her father's death.

The first time was the night when they had returned from the country after the funeral.

Kyla thought that she must be imagining the sounds that they made stumbling along the passage.

Then the door of the bedroom closed and she knew that they were both inside.

She had lain in bed awake, shocked and horrified that even her stepmother, whom she had always hated, should behave in such an outrageous fashion.

Then, before five o'clock when the housemaids came on duty, she had heard George leaving.

He was moving more quietly now because he was obviously sobering up.

He went downstairs and let himself out of the front door just as dawn was breaking.

Then she went into what had been her mother's bedroom.

She was trying not to think that the woman who had married her father would soon be occupying it with a despicable man who was prepared to go to any lengths for money.

She guessed that the fifty pounds that her stepmother had for him would still be in her handbag.

Sybil would have gone to the Bank when she was out driving today and cashed a cheque.

It was not at all difficult to find the handbag, the lady's maid had put it tidily away into a beautiful French chest of drawers inlaid with ivory.

Kyla opened it and saw that the money had been placed in one of the little canvas bags provided by the Bank.

She drew the notes out, each one ten pounds in value.

She put the money down and then went over to the French secrétaire in the corner of the bedroom.

It was where her stepmother sometimes wrote her letters.

Kyla took from it several pieces of writing paper, which was engraved with her father's crest.

She folded them neatly to the same size as the banknotes and put them into the bag.

With any luck, she thought, George Hunter would be too tired when he was ready to leave to examine very closely what he had been given.

It would be later in the day that the bomb would go off and by that time she and Terry must be far away.

She closed the drawer, picked up the five banknotes and crossed the passage to her own bedroom.

There she began to pack one of her suitcases.

She had suspected several days earlier that her stepmother would somehow contrive to be rid of her and she could not imagine how it could be done.

She had had the idea that she might be flung out of the house and sent to a Nunnery or even shipped abroad.

Now she realised in all its gory what her stepmother really intended.

She realised that she would rather die than be touched by Lord Frome whether she was drugged or not.

His outrageous behaviour had shocked even the lax and raffish Society that was centred round the King.

George IV might be a rake and continuously obsessed by one mistress after another but at least he was known as 'the First Gentleman of Europe'.

Lord Frome was a very different proposition.

Although he was usually spoken about in whispers, Kyla, without really listening, knew that he had committed unforgivable crimes.

He had pursued young women, whether they were milkmaids on his estate or very young girls who were brought from the country by the procurers of the Houses of Pleasure.

They deceived the poor girls, who were in reality little more than children and they came to London believing that there was an excellent job for them in the house of a member of the Nobility.

That was the only true part of the story. Once they were in the clutches of Lord Frome, there was no going back to the country or anywhere else except for the River Thames.

'How could anybody be as wicked as my stepmother,' Kyla often asked herself, 'and yet clever enough to have managed to take Mama's place?'

Her father had been broken-hearted when her mother had died.

Yet he had been beguiled, allured and finally possessed by Sybil.

Admittedly she was very attractive, there was no doubt about that.

Now, after what she had heard her say downstairs, Kyla was deeply suspicious.

She had not only encouraged her father to drink much more than he ever had before but perhaps she had also used drugs.

She had certainly made him seem as weak as water in her hands.

Maybe it was the drugs that George Hunter had referred to when he said that the doctors were astonished that her father had died when he was so comparatively young.

'She murdered him!' Kyla cried in her heart and wanted to confront her stepmother with the devastating truth.

Then she knew that she must not think of anything else but saving Terry.

She quickly began to pack a light bag as well as her suitcase

It was little more than a strong basket which she had brought down from the attics two days earlier.

She put into it some light easy to carry dresses that were simple.

They were not in the least like the gowns she had bought the previous year in which to make her debut.

When she had finished taking what she wanted from out of the wardrobe and the chest of drawers, she went to her dressing table.

She collected the jewellery that was hers and what was left of her mother's.

There was, in fact, very little and Sybil had rifled the safe almost immediately after she was married to Kyla's father.

She had removed the necklaces, the tiara, the bracelets, brooches and rings, which had been kept in the country.

However, when they returned to London, Kyla, by being quick-witted, had managed to get hold of what had belonged to her mother before Sybil was aware of where it was.

Sybil had expected that the jewels would be in a safe in the pantry as they had been in the country.

Kyla's mother, however, had a small safe in her bedroom and she had kept in it all the jewels that she wore every day.

They were by no means as valuable as what she called laughingly her 'State Jewels'.

But they were very beautiful and they had been presents for her birthday and Christmas from a husband who loved her adoringly.

Kyla had already packed them up and now she put them in her bag.

Then she hesitated.

At the back of a drawer there was a small case that had not been included with the rest.

She opened it and inside, lying against the velvet, was her mother's Wedding ring.

She slipped it over the third finger of her left hand.

As she did so, she felt that her mother was prompting her and telling her what to do.

She looked round, thinking that there was nothing else for her to take with her.

Then she went to the door and, as she reached it, she heard the sounds of two people coming up the stairs, making a great deal of noise as they did so.

She knew that it was her stepmother and George Hunter, drunk as they usually were.

They thought that because they were not speaking, she would not be aware of what they were doing.

They reached Sybil's bedroom and Kyla heard them closing the door.

This was a dangerous moment.

If Sybil now going to give George Hunter the money that she had procured for him, he might be aware that it was not in the little bag.

As she listened, Kyla could hear a sudden ripple of laughter.

She thought that she heard a thump, as if too unsteady to go any farther, they had thrown themselves down on the bed.

She felt a shudder go through her and she knew at once that she must wait a little while longer until they were asleep.

She moved back into her own bedroom, opening the drawers and the cupboards silently.

She was making certain that she had forgotten nothing that she would need.

She put the fifty pounds into her own handbag and with it there was the money that she had been saving up ever since her father's death.

She had known instinctively that the hatred that her stepmother had for her would make it impossible for them to live in the same house.

She had been desperately worried, if she was to be sent away, as to what would happen to Terry.

She had never in her wildest dreams imagined anything so appalling as her stepmother contriving to kill him.

But she had known after the funeral, when her father's Solicitor had read the Will, that her stepmother was seething with anger.

Lord Shenley had made it very clear that everything he possessed went with the title.

It was not an old one as titles go and in fact he had been the third Lord Shenley and now Terry was the fourth.

Before that the Shenleys, who had played their patriotic part as Statesmen and soldiers, had received various honours.

Amongst them at the beginning of the last century was a Baronetcy.

It was because Kyla's great-grandfather had been a Statesman and of personal service to King George III that he had been made a Peer so he could legislate in the House of Lords.

He had also been extremely rich, but it was most unfortunate that during the War against Napoleon, as had happened with so many families, the estate had ceased to be profitable and much money had been lost in Bank failures.

There were indeed the valuable contents of Shenley House in the country, which had been collected by the family over many centuries. But these were all entailed onto the heirs to the title.

Unfortunately, because a number of Shenleys had been killed both at sea with Nelson and on the battlefield with Wellington, there was no heir after Terry.

Sybil had been left an allowance by her father, so it had never struck Kyla for one instant that she would be greedy enough to try to obtain everything that was Terry's by right of birth.

He was a dear little boy who had arrived when Lord Shenley and his wife had almost given up any hope of having an heir.

Kyla, whom they adored, was then ten and Lady Shenley said that it had happened only because she had prayed at a sacred place on the Continent. It was a shrine where women who desired children went.

When she had returned to England, she had become aware that, like a miracle, she was carrying a child.

As if Terry must live up to the way that he had been born, he was a beautiful quiet well-behaved baby.

Everyone loved him instinctively and he was such a sweet little boy that Kyla adored her brother.

She thought that only someone who was utterly wicked could think of murdering him.

It must have been her mother and her father protecting those they loved which made her afraid for the future.

Ever since her father fell ill, she had been turning over in her mind what would happen if he died.

When he did die, from some strange illness that the doctors could not diagnose, she had been desperately afraid.

Now she knew that she had every reason to be.

It must have been God's protection that came from above that had prepared her for this moment of horror.

She knew that she somehow had to fend for herself and most importantly for Terry.

She waited until at least half-an-hour had passed by and then very very softly she crept along the passage.

Terry was sleeping three or four rooms away in the one that he always occupied when they came to London.

She went in to find that the curtains were pulled back.

She could see by the light of the moon and the stars that he was fast asleep in his small bed.

She did not wake him, but went to the wardrobe to take out the clothes that he should wear now. She also took from the drawers the things that she must pack for him.

They were not many, because she knew that they would have to carry their belongings.

It would be a mistake to have anything too heavy, which could hinder their movements.

For Terry she chose some shirts and a spare pair of trousers, colourful socks and a pair of comfortable shoes.

She packed them all in another convenient bag that she had hidden behind the wardrobe where the housemaids had not seen it.

Then at last she sat down on the side of the bed and said quietly,

"Wake up, Terry."

He tinned over, as if he had no wish to open his eyes, and she said again,

"Wake up, Terry! It is important, darling."

This roused him and he then said in a sleepy tone,

"What is the matter? Is it morning?"

"No, darling, it is still night, but we have to go away."

Terry now woke up completely.

"Go away? What do you mean, Kyla?"

"We have to leave this house. I did not tell you before, but Stepmama is plotting terrible things against us and we have to escape."

Terry sat up in his bed.

"How are we going to do that?" he asked.

Now there was a note of excitement in his voice and Kyla knew that he thought it was all an adventure.

"Everyone is asleep," she said, "and so I want you to get up and put on the clothes I have laid out for you. Don't make a noise and don't speak. When I come back, we will creep down the stairs and be far away before Stepmama wakes up."

"Where are we going?" Terry asked.

"I will tell you later," Kyla replied. "Now do exactly what I say."

She paused before she added,

"I just don't want to frighten you, but it would be a disaster and very very dangerous if Stepmama found out what we were doing and then stopped us."

Terry nodded as if he understood.

"I will be very quiet," he promised.

"Then get dressed quickly," Kyla said, "while I fetch my bag from my room."

She knew that he would do as he was told and she bent and kissed him on the cheek.

"You will have to be very brave," she urged, "as Papa would want you to be and, of course, you will have to look after me as I will look after you."

"I will do that," Terry said. "Can I have my gun?"

"I have already packed it," she answered.

Terry smiled.

As he got out of bed, Kyla slipped out through the door and crept back to her own room.

She finished putting on the clothes that she had chosen to travel in.

Then she took out from the wardrobe a cloak that had belonged to her mother and was trimmed with sable.

It had been very expensive and she knew that her stepmother had often looked at it with envious eyes.

But she felt that what she wanted at the moment was to be able to create an impression of someone of importance.

It was too warm at the moment to wear the cloak.

Yet even to carry it would make those people think that she was a Lady of Substance.

She put on an extremely pretty bonnet on which she had added a few feathers to a rather plain trimming.

Taking up her handbag, her gloves and the bag in which she had packed her clothes, she tiptoed out of the room.

She also took the key with her and then locked the door.

Again she was afraid that the sound might be heard.

Then she put the key into her handbag and crept down the passage.

She knew that in the morning, when the maid came to call her and found the door locked, she would think that she wished to sleep late.

She would go away without making any fuss that she could not get into her room.

Her stepmother always slept late until nearly noon, which was not surprising considering how late she went to bed full of alcohol.

'By the time they find that I am no longer in the house,' Kyla told herself, 'Terry and I will be far away!'

At the same time she was praying, praying that there would be no unfortunate mishaps and no unexpected disruption to the plan that was working at full speed in her mind.

She opened the door of Terry's room and saw that he was ready.

"You have come," he said in a whisper. "I thought perhaps I had been dreaming."

"You have not been dreaming," Kyla said. "Now we start a very big adventure together."

Terry picked up his bag.

They went out of the room and then down the passage until they came to a secondary staircase that led down to the kitchen quarters.

Kyla knew exactly where the staff would be sleeping.

The only danger on the ground floor was the pantry boy, who slept in the pantry so as to guard the silver in the safe.

As he was small and rather ineffective, she had always thought that any burglar would overpower him easily.

It would have been very much better to have had a dog that barked or an older man with some strength. But it was not her business to interfere with the household.

As they crept past the pantry, they could hear the boy snoring away on his rather hard bed, which folded up into the wall in the daytime.

There was, of course, no one in the kitchen and they passed the scullery and the larder before they reached the back door.

Kyla pulled back the bolts, which made only a little noise.

They then opened the door to the basement with its iron steps that led to the pavement outside.

They were not very wide and Kyla had to carry her bag in front of her while Terry ran up quite easily.

Hill Street was empty at that hour of the morning.

The stars were just beginning to fade overhead and soon the dawn would be breaking to sweep away the sable of the night.

Taking Terry by the hand, Kyla started off at a brisk pace towards the streets that led into Piccadilly.

"Where are we going?" Terry asked her.

It was the first time that he had spoken since they had left his bedroom.

"We are going to the country," Kyla answered.

"That is good," Terry said, "but will not Stepmama find us there?"

"We are not going home," Kyla replied, "that would be too dangerous. We are going to see Nanny."

"Nanny!" Terry exclaimed. "Where is she?"

"When Nanny last wrote to me, which was at Easter, she was still at Lilliecote Castle."

"Is it a long way away?" Terry asked.

"I am afraid it is," Kyla answered, "but Nanny will know what we should do and where we should go. There is no one else we can trust."

"Are we running away for ever and ever?" Terry enquired.

"We are running away from Stepmama and she must never ever be able to find us," Kyla said positively.

"She does not like me," Terry stated. "She said yesterday, when you were not there, that all children are tiresome and that I was one of the worst and I was also — obstructive."

He stumbled over the word.

Kyla knew exactly what her stepmother had meant by that and what she intended to do about it.

Her fingers tightened on her brother's.

"You are neither of those things," she said. "It is only because Stepmama is a wicked woman that she dislikes anyone who is good and you have always been very good, Terry."

"I have tried to be," Terry said. "It has not been easy at school."

He had been at a day school, which was why her stepmother had got rid of Nanny.

~25~

There had really been no excuse that Terry was too old to have a Nanny and Kyla had thought that it was actually because Nanny would not allow Sybil to say unkind things about Terry or herself.

Nanny had been with them for over ten years and she had come first to look after Kyla when her own Nanny was too old and wished to retire.

She had then been delighted and thrilled when Terry was born and she had a baby to look after.

She had loved them both and they had loved her.

Kyla had wept bitterly when her stepmother had sent Nanny away.

"Now that Terry goes to a school," she had pronounced in a lofty tone, "he has no need for a Nanny and would doubtless be teased for having one."

She paused a moment and had then gone on,

"Now that Kyla has a lady's maid, it is not good for her always to be mooning about the nursery as if she was not grown up."

Ever since Nanny had gone, she had written to them regularly and had sent them small presents.

Kyla knew well that the one person who would indeed hide them and, if necessary defy her stepmother in her plan to kill them, would be Nanny.

'If she cannot have us,' she told herself, 'she will find us somewhere safe to go.'

They walked on and at last they came to the Livery stables in Piccadilly.

Kyla, holding her fur-trimmed cape tightly so that it could be seen, swept in with what she hoped was a grand air.

As it was so early in the morning, there was only a sleepy boy on duty.

"Will you please fetch the proprietor," Kyla demanded in a commanding voice.

"'E be asleep, ma'am," the boy replied.

"Then go and wake him up! Tell him that the Countess of Strafford wishes to speak to him immediately."

The boy was clearly impressed with the title.

"I'll go tell him, ma'am," he said and hurried away into the darkness.

As they waited, dawn broke over London.

They could see a long line of stalls where the Livery horses were housed.

Carriages of different sorts and makes stood in the centre of the yard.

Nearly ten minutes passed before the proprietor, looking somewhat tousled and heavy-eyed, came hurrying towards them.

"'Tis early, my Lady, for anyone to be callin'," he said, "and I was havin' a bit of shut-eye."

"I quite understand," Kyla replied, "but I have a very urgent call to go to the country and my own coachman has unfortunately been given leave of absence to attend a funeral."

"That be unfortunate, my Lady," the proprietor commented.

"What I require," Kyla continued, "is two of your best horses and a post chaise that is light and will go swiftly. My son and I have to be in Berkhamsted with all possible speed."

"I'll do me best, my Lady," the proprietor said, "but it'll cost you more than if you 'ad your own carriage."

He said this as a joke and Kyla did not laugh but merely went on sharply,

"I want your best horses."

"I'll see to that," the Proprietor answered.

He hurried away and Kyla thought that she had been very lucky.

The money that her stepmother had intended to give to George Hunter would now pay for everything she required.

After all it really belonged to Terry, but she doubted if her stepmother would appreciate that.

The two horses she saw were young and they looked fresh.

They were put between the shafts of a light up to date post-chaise.

A driver was hurriedly awakened and appeared yawning.

He announced, in a voice that Kyla could not help overhearing, that he was hungry and did not like driving before he had his breakfast.

"I daresay 'er Ladyship'll want to stop for a snack," the proprietor suggested.

"I 'opes so," the driver replied.

He climbed into the driving seat and the carriage drew up in front of Kyla.

Then the proprietor asked her for what she knew was quite a large sum even for a good post-chaise.

"I certainly hope," she said a little scathingly, "that your horses are as good as the price you value them at."

"You can be certain of that, my Lady," the Proprietor said confidently.

Kyla paid him the money and let him see, the roll of notes that she had taken it from.

He bowed respectfully and, after their bags had been strapped on behind, they drove off.

Only as the horses next turned into Piccadilly did Kyla think, with an elation that was irrepressible, that they had won, at least for the moment.

They had got away!

They had escaped!

Unless they were very unlucky, their stepmother would find it impossible to trace them.

'Thank You, God, *thank You*,' she said in her heart and added,

'I hope Mama and Papa are looking after us. It is going to be very difficult to manage on our own.'

CHAPTER TWO

They stopped for a quick luncheon in a small village at a pretty black and white inn on the village green.

"Do you think that Stepmama will follow us here?" Terry asked nervously.

"I am praying she will be deceived by the way we are covering our tracks," Kyla replied. "But we must be careful because she is our Guardian by Law and could compel us to come back to her."

Terry, realising what this meant, exclaimed,

"She is hateful! Why did Papa ever marry her?"

"That is something I have often asked myself," Kyla admitted.

As a matter of fact she suspected that Sybil had used underhand methods, perhaps even drugs, in the same way as she was prepared to use them on her.

Certainly her father had drunk a great deal more than he ever had before Sybil became his wife and Kyla felt quite certain that his death had not been a natural one.

She looked at her beloved brother, praying desperately that he would be safe.

He was such a dear little boy, so unspoilt and so unaware of the evil and horrible things that happened in the outside world.

It was unthinkable that he should become the victim of a woman like their stepmother.

Because she was so eager to move on, Kyla ate hurriedly and the bill, when it did come, was quite a small one, even including their driver's meal.

Then they were off again.

It was now late in the afternoon when they finally arrived at Berkhamsted, a small town on the main highway.

And Kyla went into the Posting inn, looking impressive in her feather bonnet.

"I am the Countess of Stafford," she declared, "and I require a room for myself and one adjacent for my son."

"Of course, your Ladyship," the proprietor said, bowing, "and we'll do our best to make your visit comfortable."

She was shown into what Kyla guessed was the best bedroom in the inn.

It was certainly comfortable and the room next door for Terry had a communicating door with hers.

She felt that they would both find this reassuring.

When they went downstairs for dinner, Kyla found that the meal was well cooked and appetising.

She was glad, however, that there were few other guests staying there.

When she went upstairs before dinner, she had sent for her maid to help her take off her gown and enquired,

"This is a charming inn, but it is surely not the only one in town?"

"Oh, no, my Lady," the maid replied, "there be another one, but it's not patronised by the Gentry like this one. Though they says as the 'orses be as good as ours."

Kyla had found out what she wanted to know and so changed the subject.

Terry was tired, having been woken in the middle of the night and she herself had had no sleep.

So she was exhausted by the time that dinner was finished.

Just as they were about to leave the dining room, the proprietor said,

"The driver of your post-chaise, my Lady, wants to know if you'll still be requirin' 'is services tomorrow, otherwise 'e'll take 'is horses 'ome."

"Tell him we have friends who are meeting us here and he can therefore leave whenever it suits him," Kyla replied.

She paused and then continued,

"But ask him to come and see me since I would like to give him something for himself."

The proprietor hurried away.

When the driver of the post-chaise came to see her, Kyla told him in a loud voice that her friends were collecting them the next morning.

She felt that those overhearing the conversation would repeat every word if any enquiries were made.

She tipped him well and he thanked her profusely and she also complimented him on his driving.

When they were upstairs and the maid had left the room, Terry asked,

"Have we really got friends coming to meet us, Kyla?"

"No, not really," Kyla replied, "but if anyone asks it is what the driver will tell them."

"Then what are we going to do?" Terry wanted to know.

He was obviously very tired and Kyla thought that he was behaving extremely well in the circumstances.

"Just between ourselves," she said in a low voice, "we are going to the other Posting inn, where we will hire a carriage under a different name, which will take us on to the next place where we will stay tomorrow night."

"And where will we find Nanny?" Terry asked.

"She is a little further on," Kyla explained, "but we have to be very very careful, Terry, just in case anyone has followed us. Of course they will be enquiring about a 'young woman on her own with a boy'."

"They must not catch us," Terry said anxiously.

"No, of course not," Kyla replied. "And we must pray very hard that we have been clever enough to deceive them."

She went with him to his bedroom and tucked him in for the night.

He put his arms around her neck.

"It is a very exciting adventure, is it not, Kyla?" he asked.

"Very exciting," she agreed. And you have to help me."

"I will," Terry said, "but I think I ought to have my gun with me."

"You shall have your gun when it is necessary," Kyla said. "For the moment it is quite safe in my bag."

She knew as she spoke that they had been very lucky that a long time ago their father had taught them both how to shoot. He had first taught his wife and then the children.

"When we are travelling," he then had explained, "you will meet all sorts of unpleasant people making trouble and I think that every woman should know how to protect herself."

"I have no need to do that when I have you beside me, darling," Lady Shenley had said.

"I know that, my precious," he had replied, "but I might not always be here and I want you to feel safe wherever you happen to be."

He had put his arms around his wife and kissed her.

Kyla remembered how her mother had learnt to be a first class shot, hitting the bullseye every time.

It had taken Kyla a little longer.

Then, of course, Terry had wanted to learn more.

"It's not fair, Papa," he had wailed. "I am a man and if you were not here, I would have to protect Mama and Kyla."

"Of course you would," his father had agreed. "I tell you what I will do. I am going off to London tomorrow and I will find you a pistol that will be the right size for you."

Terry, who had been only six at the time, had given a whoop of joy.

Lord Shenley was as good as his word.

He had found for his son a pistol which had once belonged to a Russian Princess. It was very small with a jewelled holster, but the pistol itself was workmanlike.

Although it was not likely to kill anyone, it could make a very nasty wound if an animal or a man should threaten Terry.

He had practised diligently until he too became a good shot.

When he had hit three bullseyes in succession, he was wildly excited.

"I have done it! I have done it, Papa!" he cried. "Now you have to call me a 'first class shot' just like you."

"I am really proud of you, my boy," his father said, "and when you are older you shall have a weapon the same size as mine."

Kyla bade Terry 'goodnight' and went to her own room.

She could not help hoping that they would never have to use their pistols against anyone.

It seemed totally incredible that any woman would deliberately plan to kill a small boy, especially one as delightful and charming as her brother.

'I have to save him, I *have* to,' she told herself forcefully.

She longed for the night to pass quickly so that they could once again be on their way.

*

The next morning Kyla woke Terry very early.

As they went down to breakfast, she doubted that the proprietor would be about at that hour of the morning.

She was right in her assumption as there was only one sleepy waitress and an even more sleepy porter on duty.

After they had eaten, Kyla handed the porter some money, saying,

"Please give this to the innkeeper for me. Tell him that we spent a comfortable night, but have to leave early as a carriage is coming for us from a friend's house. It will be here by eight o'clock as we have a long way to go."

The porter was not particularly interested.

But, as Kyla had tipped him, she thought that he would remember what she had said.

Carrying their bags, Kyla and Terry hurriedly left the inn.

"Where are we really going?" Tory asked.

"We are going to the other inn," Kyla answered, "but now we will have a different name and I am your Governess. When you hear what I will tell them when we reach it, don't be surprised."

Again, as it was still early in the morning, there was only a young groom in attendance in the stables of the next inn.

"I hope you can help me," Kyla said. "I am Miss Brown and the Governess of this young gentleman, who is the son of Sir Thomas Brampton. Unfortunately the carriage in which we were travelling was involved in a slight accident and the wheel is buckled. As I have no wish to wait for it to be repaired, I would like to hire a vehicle to carry us as quickly as possible to Royston."

This was a town which she knew they could easily reach by that evening.

The groom scratched his head.

"I don't know as I can give you a post-chaise," he said, "without me askin' the Head Groom."

"Then go and ask him at once," Kyla said, "as Lady Brampton is eagerly awaiting our arrival."

The lad hurried away and, as she expected, the proprietor was impressed by the assumed title.

When he arrived, Kyla. told her story and made it clear that there was no time to be lost.

Almost quicker than she could believe it, they were on the road again.

The post-chaise was not as comfortable as the one that they had ridden in the previous day.

The two horses, however, seemed young and fresh and that was all that mattered.

Once again they stopped for luncheon, but the inn was full of noisy men.

They looked at Kyla in a way that made her feel embarrassed and she was glad when it was time to leave.

She then decided that it was a mistake to stop at inns where there were a lot of people.

For tomorrow, she thought, she would order luncheon to take with them from wherever they stayed the night.

It was a long and tiring journey even though they were on a main road all of the time.

In fact it was so tiring that in the afternoon Terry fell asleep as he cuddled up to Kyla.

She put her arms around him and thought of the future and how she must take her brother to safety.

She was wondering what was happening at the house in London and what her stepmother had said when it was discovered that they were both missing.

'She will be very angry,' Kyla told herself, 'but she will not dare to go to the Police in case they find us and we tell them why we ran away.'

At the same time she could not be certain of anything.

Quite suddenly she felt very young and vulnerable and so alone in the world that it was becoming more and more frightening.

'Help me, Mama, help me, Papa,' she prayed. 'I am frightened – very very frightened.'

Because the horses had grown tired, it was late in the evening when they finally reached the Posting inn at Royston.

It was in no way as comfortable as the one that they had previously slept in.

Nevertheless the beds were clean and no one seemed to take any interest in them, but Kyla told herself that the less notice the proprietor took of her and Terry the better.

There was a badly cooked unappetising dinner, during which Terry almost fell asleep at the table.

At last they were in their beds and Kyla thought with relief that there was only one more day to go.

She kept going over and over in her mind what lay ahead.

She recognised that it would be a great mistake to arrive at Lilliecote Castle without first warning Nanny that they were travelling under assumed names.

She did not underestimate her stepmother's brain and it was more than possible that she would remember how fond they had been of Nanny.

It might in fact be the first place she would look if she was desperately intent on finding them.

Although Kyla was very tired, she lay awake for a long time, planning out what she must do.

*

The next morning before she left the inn Kyla asked where the stagecoach stopped on the main road.

It was a question that the people in the inn were used to hearing.

Only a few of their guests came in their own carriages or could afford a post-chaise.

She was told not only where the stagecoach stopped but also the route that it followed.

Kyla knew that it would take them within two miles of Lilliecote Castle.

They walked from the inn to the coach stop and Kyla was relieved to find that there was only one farmer's wife waiting.

She was carrying a basket containing eggs and two dead chickens that had not been plucked.

When the stagecoach arrived, Terry begged to be allowed to sit on top and as there were only two men on the coach, Kyla allowed him to do so.

She climbed inside.

There were two other women, both of them obviously farmers' wives like the one who they had waited with her for the stagecoach.

She thought it important for her to arouse no particular interest, so she sat quietly in her corner and looked out of the window.

The farmers' wives chatted endlessly to each other about how expensive everything was these days and they also complained that they received so little for their farm produce.

Kyla thought that it was an old story that had been repeated over and over again.

At the same time she could understand how much they resented their difficulties, which had been created by cheap food imported into the country from the Continent of Europe and it had undercut the prices of home-grown produce.

It was just on noon when they came to a coach stop, which she knew was only about two miles from The Castle.

She then jumped out of the coach, saying a shy 'farewell' to the other occupants and they responded without showing any interest.

Terry climbed down from the top of the coach, saying as it drove off,

"That was spiffing, Kyla! I liked it up there."

"I thought you would," Kyla said as she smiled, "and now we have a long way to walk and I expect you are hungry. I am very glad I brought some sandwiches for our luncheon. We will have it quite soon."

She had told the maid that was what she wanted when they went down to breakfast.

They did not look very appetising and yet, at least, she thought it would sustain them until they reached Nanny.

She was quite certain that once that happened, Nanny would want to feed Terry up and her too.

"I would like a drink," Terry asked.

"So would I," Kyla agreed, "but I think it would be a mistake to be seen in any of the village inns near to The Castle. We had better find Nanny first and arrange how we can hide."

"Do you mean we have to hide even when we are with Nanny?" Terry asked.

Kyla nodded.

"I am sure that Stepmama will look for us here."

'If she tries to take us away, I will shoot her," Terry asserted.

The way he spoke made Kyla remember the pistols they had in their bags.

It, however, did seem to be rather a far-fetched situation.

At the same time her father had warned her so often about keeping their pistols beside them. But it would have been stupid to be caught defenceless.

What money she had left was very precious and it had to be spent wisely.

She then rose to her feet and, going under a tree, undid her baggage.

She felt for her own pistol, which she put into her pocket.

Then she took out Terry's smaller one.

"Now I can protect you," Terry said valiantly, "and, if anyone comes to take us back to Stepmama, I will shoot them!"

"You must remember that our Papa said we were never to shoot unless it was absolutely necessary," Kyla replied, "and I, for one, have no wish to kill anyone."

"I would not kill them," Terry said after thinking for a moment. "I would shoot them in the leg or maybe the arm, so that they could not run away."

Kyla drew in her breath.

It was something she did not want to think about. Instead she concentrated on how they could reach Lilliecote Castle and talk to Nanny without anyone being aware of it.

She tied up her baggage again and they set off, finding it hard going over a rough field.

Kyla knew by the map she had studied when planning the journey that they were going in the right direction.

They had left the main road as soon as the stagecoach had disappeared out of sight.

Now, as they turned to the left, bearing West, they would fairly soon, she reckoned, see The Castle in the distance.

Nanny had written in many of her letters to them, just how impressive The Castle was and that it could be seen for miles around as it was built on the top of a hill.

She had written,

"It has been in the Earl's family for hundreds of years and I know that both you and Terry would find it exciting because it has secret passages. There are many beautiful rooms, some of which were added after The Castle was first built."

'Perhaps we could hide in the secret passages,' Kyla thought, but did not say it aloud.

She knew that mentioning it would make Terry determined to do so, whether there was danger or not.

They walked on, until they came to some trees overlooking a small valley.

Kyla knew that they had to descend to a stream that ran through it and then up again on the other side.

She sank down onto the ground.

"Let's have something to eat now," she proposed. "I am finding my baggage very much heavier than I expected."

"So is mine," Terry said, "and I am hungry."

She opened the parcel of sandwiches and she found that they were not as unpleasant as she had anticipated they might be.

The bread was fresh and had been spread with butter and the pieces of ham that filled it were quite edible.

Terry started to eat the sandwiches with delight.

He was just telling Kyla again how hungry he was when she heard the sound of a horse coming up behind them.

Turning round, she gave a gasp of horror.

The man riding the horse had a handkerchief over the lower part of his face and there was a large pistol in his hand.

She stared at him in terror.

Then, before either she or the highwayman could speak, Terry pulled out his pistol.

The movement of his hand made Kyla remember hers and, taking her pistol from out of her pocket, she pointed it at the intruder.

He stared at the two of them for a moment and then very unexpectedly he laughed.

"I don't believe it!" he exclaimed loudly, looking at Terry. "Is that pistol for real?"

"Very real," Kyla said in a voice that shook a little, "as you will see if you try to make demands on us."

"Now, what would two children of your age be a-doin' with pistols?" the highwayman laughed again.

He put his own weapon back into his pocket and went on,

"I reckons there's a story behind all this. Put them dangerous weapons away and if you can spare I a bit to eat, that's all I'll make you deliver."

The way he spoke was so friendly that Kyla lowered her pistol.

Only Terry kept his pointed firmly at the highwayman.

The man next knotted the reins on his horse's neck.

It was then that Kyla realised that it was a very fine stallion, so fine that she was sure it was unusual for a highwayman, of all people, to own such a magnificent horse.

"Where did you get such a wonderful mount?" she asked him impulsively.

"Where d'you think?" the highwayman laughed. "I stole 'im!"

He patted the horse on its back and it moved away, lowering its head to crop the grass.

The highwayman pulled down the handkerchief from his face and sat down beside them under the trees.

"Now, what be you two up to?" he enquired. "I'm bettin' you've run away from school."

'It is much worse than that," Kyla answered. "We are in danger and very frightened, so please don't make it any worse for us than it is already."

"Of course I won't," the highwayman replied, scratching his nose.

He glanced at Terry, who was still standing there with the small pistol in his hand.

"Put the gun away, Sonny," he said, "but you're quite right to protect this pretty lady, who I sees be older than I thinks 'er was."

Kyla handed the highwayman a sandwich and he took it gratefully.

"I be ever so 'ungry," he said. "I've 'ad a couple of real bad days and the only money I 'as goes on the 'orse's food and not mine."

Kyla was thinking that he was not such a bad man after all.

No man who would put his horse before his own needs could be cruel.

"Did you really steal him?" she asked.

"'Course I did," the highwayman admitted. "It was a real fair do. I left me own 'orse in exchange, though 'e's a bit long in the tooth and much slower than Samson."

"Is that his name?" Terry asked. 'It's a good name for a horse."

"That's what I thinks," the highwayman agreed. "Now tell me what be you two young 'uns up to?"

"As I told you, we are in deadly danger," Kyla replied.

"Then what be you a-doin' 'ere?"

Kyla paused and then somehow she knew instinctively that she could trust this man.

He might be a highwayman, but at the same time he looked kind and fatherly.

Anyway it was difficult to think that he could ever be murderous.

"We are trying to get to Lilliecote Castle," she said, "where we have a friend. We don't, however, want anybody to know that we are there until we actually see our friend inside The Castle."

"That sounds a bit complicated," the highwayman admitted, "but I gets your meanin'. Well, I suppose I'll 'ave to 'elp you then."

"Could you do that?" Kyla asked. "We would be so very very grateful."

She passed him another sandwich as she spoke, which he accepted without speaking.

After a long pause he said,

"I've done all sorts of things in me life, but I 'as me principles as no doubt you 'ave yours."

"Of course we have – " Kyla answered.

"Why are you a highwayman?" Terry interrupted. "If you are caught, you will be hanged from a gibbet."

"That's why I 'as to keep on goin'," the highwayman replied, "and now I've got Samson, it's not so difficult."

"You mean you can get away quickly?" Kyla asked.

"Aye, that's the long and the short of it, but I suspects they'll get I in the end."

"Tell me," Kyla asked him, "so why are you a highwayman?"

"I were a good gardener," he replied, "and I 'ad green fingers with flowers, they used to say, but it be not difficult for me, I guess. I comes back 'avin' served me King and Country, so to speak, and what do I find? Me job's gone, me wife's run off with another man and me cottage be occupied by another family. That's 'ow they treats 'eroes!"

"I agree with you. It is disgraceful the way that our soldiers and sailors have been left to starve, especially those

~47~

who were wounded," Kyla said. "It made my father very angry."

"It made I very angry too!" the highwayman said. "So I takes to the road and somehow enjoys meself. "Though you may not think so, at least I be free. For the moment.""

"You will have to be very careful," Terry warned him.

"I am," he replied. "But I never expects I'd find two babes in arms flashing pistols at I!"

He laughed until he choked and then he carried on,

"Anyway, it's nice to meet you and if you be wantin' go to The Castle, I'll give you a lift."

"On Samson?" Terry asked excitedly.

"On Samson," the highwayman affirmed. "He be strong enough to carry the three of us."

"Are you sure you don't mind?" Kyla asked. "It is very kind of you and it was very hot when we were walking."

"'Course it be. Now give me your baggage, miss."

He took it from them and fixed it firmly in a clever way to Samson's saddle.

Then he put Terry up in front of him and, having mounted, pulled Kyla up behind him.

She put her arms round his waist to keep herself steady.

They set off, moving between the trees and, she was quite certain seen by no one.

They had gone for some distance when he stopped and announced,

"Here us be. That's what you be a-lookin' for."

He pointed and Kyla could see ahead of them silhouetted against the sky the Towers and roofs of what appeared to be a very large building.

"Is that The Castle?" Terry asked excitedly. "It looks spiffing! I have never been inside a Castle before."

"You enjoy it whilst you 'as the chance," the highwayman said, "but if you 'as to get away in an 'urry, remember if I'm anywhere near 'ere I'll 'elp you out."

"You are very kind," Kyla said. "Could you not find a better job than holding up people on the highway?"

"Don't you worry your pretty little 'ead about I. Jest you take care of yourself and if you be in danger, real danger, you can always get in touch with I."

"What is your name?" Kyla asked. "And how can I possibly contact you?"

The highwayman thought for a moment.

And then he said,

"There be a very large oak tree in the Park, as everyone in the village believes 'as magic powers and can 'elp when you're in trouble or when you be ill. Anyone can tell you where it be."

He paused for a few moments as if he was thinking out what he was just about to say.

"Now what you must do is to put a small red kerchief round one of the boughs of the oak tree at dusk. There be all sorts of charms and little things left there, but I ain't never seen a red kerchief. A red ribbon'll do if you ain't got no kerchief."

"Then what will happen?" Kyla asked.

"I'll wait for you at the tree when there be no one about and you can tell I what's amiss."

"Thank you – *thank you!*" Kyla sighed. "It is so very kind of you."

The highwayman thought for a moment.

Then he went on,

"If things gets too 'ot for me and I 'as to go away quickly, I wouldn't want you to be disappointed if I didn't show up."

"Then what should I do?" Kyla asked.

"Well, if it so 'appens," he said, "I'll leave sommat on a bough for you. It might be jest a bit of Samson's mane, but it'll tell you that I can't meet you that night."

"I will certainly go to the tree every day," Kyla said. "I would like to see it anyway"

"So would I," Terry smiled a toothy smile.

The highwayman brought Samson to a standstill.

"I'll not take you any further," he said. "It's only a short walk to The Castle from 'ere."

"I think we shall have to hide somewhere in the garden," Kyla said, "hoping the person I am waiting to see will come out of The Castle and I can have a chance to speak to her alone."

The highwayman urged Samson forward and, when he stopped again, he said,

"If you walk from 'ere and go straight through the shrubbery, then you peeps through the bushes, you'll see the lawns and the Bowling Green ahead of you

"Thank you, *thank you*!" Kyla said. "You are the kindest man we have ever met and I am so grateful to you."

"It were nice talkin' to you," he replied in a gruff voice. "It ain't often I gets a chance of speakin' to a beautiful young lady like you be. I 'ad a daughter meself once, but 'er died after I'd gone to the War."

"I am sorry," Kyla said sympathetically.

Then she put up her hand to lay it on his.

"I think perhaps your daughter is glad that we met you and that you have been able to help us."

"That be a real good thing for you to say," the highwayman replied, turning away.

But Kyla had already seen that there was a hint of moisture in his eyes.

He turned to Terry.

"Now, young feller, you look after this pretty lady as I guess 'er must be your sister and don't you let anyone 'arm 'er."

"I will shoot them if they try!" Terry replied aggressively.

"Of course you will," the highwayman agreed, "but see you aim straight!"

He then released their bags from the saddle and, as they fell to the ground, he pulled on Samson's reins.

"'Bye," he called out. "And don't forget, if anythin' bad 'appens, leave a message on the old oak."

"I will not forget," Kyla said, "and thank you, thank you again so very much."

She paused before she then asked hesitatingly,

"I would like to have – a name when I – think of you, but perhaps it is wrong for me to ask."

The highwayman smiled.

"I'll tell you. 'Bill' is what me friends, when I 'ad some, called me."

"Then I will call you 'Bill' when I pray that you will be safe," Kyla said.

"You do that, miss," the highwayman replied.

"And when you think of us," Kyla said, "I am 'Kyla' and my brother is 'Terry', but no one must know we are here."

"I'll keep me mouth closed."

He lifted his hat and, as he did so, Kyla saw that he was going grey.

As he put it on again, Samson carried him away quickly and they disappeared amongst the trees.

Terry gave a sigh.

"Fancy our meeting a real live highwayman!" he exclaimed. "I wish I could tell the boys at school. They would never believe it."

"You must promise me that you will tell no one or we will get him into trouble," Kyla said quickly. "If there are people looking for us, there will certainly be people looking for him too."

"Yes, of course," Terry said, "but he was nice, was he not, Kyla?"

"Very nice," Kyla nodded.

They picked up their baggage and started to walk through some trees that gradually gave way to shrubs.

Many of them were in bloom and there was a fragrance in the air that was very attractive.

Kyla moved on cautiously as she had no wish to be found by a gardener, who would ask her what they were doing here.

Then, through the bushes just ahead of her, she could see green lawns.

To the right, as the highwayman had told them, there was the Bowling Green.

Now that she was closer to The Castle, it was even larger and more magnificent than it had seemed from a distance.

The walls were thick and sturdy with battlements.

She thought, if they stayed there, even her stepmother would not be able to harm them.

Then she told herself that this was just 'wishful thinking'.

She had to find Nanny, who might think that it would be wiser for them to go somewhere else where nobody knew them.

Her spirits dropped at the thought.

Then, as they stared up to the top of The Castle, seeing its turrets and Towers, Terry said suddenly in a whisper,

"Look, look, Kyla! There is Nanny! I can see her."

He was speaking excitedly and he would have run forward.

But Kyla put her hand out to detain him.

"Wait, wait," she said also in a whisper. "We must wait until we can speak to her out of sight of The Castle."

CHAPTER THREE

Kyla waited until Nanny had reached the Bowling Green.

Then, when she thought that she would be concealed from the house by a box hedge, she took her restraining hand from Terry's shoulder.

He sprang forward and ran through the bushes to Nanny, throwing his arms round her neck when he reached her.

"Nanny, *Nanny*," he cried, "We have come to you to save us."

Nanny looked at him in bewilderment.

Then, as Kyla joined them, she said,

"Miss Kyla! Whatever are you both doin' here?"

"We want you to help us, Nanny," Kyla replied. "And I have so much to tell you."

As she spoke, she looked at the little girl standing beside Nanny.

"We have run away," Terry told her. "And as we were very very frightened, we came to you."

"Now, I don't know what frightened you," Nanny said, "but you've done the right thing in comin' to me, both of you."

"I thought that was what you would say," Kyla informed her in a low voice.

Nanny smoothed back Terry's hair from his forehead and said,

"You have become a big boy since I last saw you."

"I am big enough to find my way here with Kyla," Terry said, "and I saved her from a highwayman."

"You'll have to tell me all about it," Nanny answered. "But first I think you must meet Lady Jane, whom I look after, and I'm sure she's a-wantin' to meet you."

She turned to the little girl beside her, who held out her hand.

"Did you really meet a – highwayman?" she asked excitedly.

"I will tell you all about it," Terry said, "and Nanny will think I was very brave."

Nanny looked at Kyla in a rather bewildered manner.

"I have so much to tell you, Nanny," she said quietly, "but it is for you alone."

Nanny took charge in the way she had always done ever since she had looked after Kyla as a baby.

"What you must do, Jane," she said, "is take Terry to see your house in the trees and, if you run ahead, Miss Kyla and I'll come along slowly."

"A house in the trees?" Terry exclaimed. "I would like to see that."

Jane held out her hand.

"I will show it to you," she said. "It is my own secret place. Even the gardeners are not allowed to go there."

"That is just what we want," Terry enthused looking at Kyla.

Then, as Jane began to move away, he ran after her.

As soon as they were out of earshot, Nanny said sharply,

"Now, what is all this about, Miss Kyla? And why have you come to see me without any warning?"

"We have come," Kyla said in a low voice, "because Stepmama – "

"I knew it would be something to do with her Ladyship!" Nanny interrupted. "If she has turned you out, I know your father, that good kind man, would turn in his grave."

"She has not turned us out," Kyla replied. "We have run away because she is planning to kill Terry and drug me!"

Nanny stared at her in amazement.

"If I wasn't aware that you have never told me a lie," she said, "I would find that hard to believe."

"It is true, Nanny, it is true" Kyla insisted. "I eavesdropped when Mr. George Hunter, whom Stepmama is in love with, came back from trying to find out how she could get her hands on all the money that Papa left for Terry."

"I suppose there is no way that she can get it legally," Nanny queried tartly.

"Apparently none," Kyla replied, "unless Terry is dead and I am disposed of."

"If ever there was a wicked woman," Nanny exclaimed, "it's her Ladyship! But I can hardly believe she'd resort to murder."

"It depends what you mean by murder," Kyla said. "But she suggested that small boys can easily fall off a roof or drown in a lake and no one would think it in any way surprising."

"So that is what she's plannin'," Nanny replied in a low voice.

"I am to be drugged," Kyla went on, "and sold to a wicked man called Lord Frome, who would take me to France, where no one would ask questions about my having disappeared."

"I can hardly believe what I'm hearin'," Nanny said. "Not even about a woman I'd not trust to cross the road in a straight line."

"When I overheard what she was planning," Kyla continued, "I took from her handbag some money that she was going to give Mr. George Hunter and then we came to you."

"Do you not think her Ladyship'll guess that you are here?" Nanny asked.

Kyla explained how she felt that they had covered their tracks by hiring two different post-chaises and ending up in the stagecoach.

"That was clever of you," Nanny said. "But now you're here. I'm thinkin' what I can do about it."

"If you cannot – keep us," Kyla said, "perhaps you will think of somewhere we can go where Stepmama will not – find us."

"How can I let you go wanderin' about the world and lookin' as you do?" Nanny asked almost beneath her breath. "And if she wants you back, she'll have the Law on her side."

"I know that," Kyla said, "but I could not stay and wait for her to kill Terry and then give me drugs so I would not know what I was doing."

Even as she spoke, Kyla felt suddenly helpless.

She looked at Nanny as a child would do, thinking in some miraculous way she would be able to save them.

As Nanny did not speak, she said after a moment,

"Please – Nanny – please think of something."

"Of course I'll think of somethin'," Nanny said sharply. "You don't suppose I would let that woman hurt my babies, whom I've always loved."

She spoke so firmly that Kyla felt tears come into her eyes and they were tears of relief.

"What – can we – do?" she asked Nanny after a moment.

"I am thinkin'," Nanny said, moving slowly forward over the Bowling Green.

"I am sure you will think of something," Kyla sighed.

"I have to," Nanny replied. 'There's no doubt, if you are missing, that woman'll make enquiries as to whether you and Terry are here."

"What if she asks the little girl's father," Kyla said hesitatingly.

"If you are talkin' about his Lordship, the Earl," Nanny replied, "he's not Lady Jane's father but her uncle. His Lordship's not married."

"You did not explain that in any of your letters," Kyla replied, "so, of course, I imagined that you were with a married couple and looking after their children."

She thought as she spoke that perhaps it was easier if there was not a lady in The Castle and she would doubtless have been more curious than a man.

"There's one good thing," Nanny said as if she was thinking about it. "His Lordship's abroad at the moment and a number of the household are havin' their holidays."

"Are you suggesting," Kyla asked, "that we might stay here with you?"

"Of course you will stay with me," Nanny said. "The difficulty'll be to keep anyone from knowing that Terry has his father's title and that you're his sister."

She walked on a little further.

Then, as she reached a clump of bushes beyond which there were some trees on rising ground, she stopped.

"I know exactly who you'll be, Miss Kyla," she said.

Kyla looked at her with wide eyes and she went on,

"I spoke to his Lordship's secretary a few weeks ago about her little Ladyship havin' lessons with someone more qualified to teach her than I am myself."

She paused for a moment before she continued,

"He said he would see if there was anyone in the neighbourhood who would come in two or three times a week. But now he's on holiday and I think it would be possible to persuade his Lordship to have a Nursery Governess in The Castle itself."

"Do you mean – *me*?" Kyla asked.

"I mean you," Nanny said firmly. "You know as well as I do that you can teach a child of seven and do it better than any ordinary Governess ever could."

Kyla smiled.

"I will certainly try. But what about Terry?"

"Now, that is more difficult," Nanny admitted.

Then she gave a little cry.

"I have it! It has come into my head like a message from the stars."

"What has?" Kyla asked.

"I had a letter just a week ago from Lady Blessingham, whom I had written to when your stepmother threw me out and claimed that Terry was too old to need a Nanny."

There was a bitter note in Nanny's voice as she spoke.

It told Kyla that she had not forgotten just how much it had upset her when she had to leave Terry and the house where she had been so happy when their mother was alive.

"What did Lady Blessingham say?" Kyla asked.

"Her Ladyship asked me how I was and said that one day she hoped to bring over her grandson to see me, who was getting on for nine."

Kyla looked at her excitedly.

"You mean that you could pretend that Terry is Lady Blessingham's grandson so that if Stepmama makes enquiries here, no one will think that he is his real self."

"That's what I mean," Nanny agreed. "We have first to convince the staff. You know how they all talk."

"Yes, of course," Kyla murmured.

"Who has seen you since you arrived here?" Nanny enquired.

"No one," Kyla answered. "And I thought it would be best if we could talk to you in the garden before we went into The Castle itself."

"That was very sensible of you," Nanny said approvingly. "Where's your luggage, if you have any?"

"It is in the bushes," Kyla said. "There are only two light bags because I knew we would have to carry them."

"Now wait a moment," Nanny said, "while I think this out. We've got to do it cleverly."

She stood still as she spoke.

Looking at her, Kyla thought that she had stepped back into the days when Nanny had been the compassionate Ruler of the nursery.

Then everything had run smoothly as if on greased wheels and there never seemed to be any problems in those days.

The nursery was always full of sunshine and she and Terry would run downstairs to the drawing room where her mother was waiting for them.

She would smile and hold out her arms for them the moment they appeared.

'We were so happy,' Kyla thought, 'and we were surrounded by love until Mama died.'

Nanny was just the same as she had always been.

'The Rock of Gibraltar', she remembered that her mother had once called her and it was exactly what she was to them at this moment.

Nanny drew in her breath.

"I've thought it out," she said, "and I knows what you have to do."

"What is it?" Kyla asked.

"I want you to go back the way you've come without bein' seen," Nanny said, "and pick up the two pieces of luggage that belong to you and to Terry."

Kyla was listening wide-eyed and Nanny then went on,

"You enter the drive when there's no one about and put your bags down beside one of the trees. I'm goin' to collect the two children and bring them to where you'll be hidin'."

"Why are we doing that?" Kyla asked. "I don't understand."

"What I'm goin' to tell Mr. Jeffreys, the butler, when I reach the house, and he's quite a sensible man, is that while Lady Jane and I were out, Lady Blessingham came by with her grandson."

"In a carriage?" Kyla asked.

"Of course in a carriage," Nanny answered. "When she saw me, she stopped and told me that she was comin' here not only to see me but to ask his Lordship if her grandson could stay with me for a few days while she goes to visit her sister, who's been taken ill."

"That is so clever of you, Nanny," Kyla exclaimed.

"I thought you'd think so," Nanny replied. "All Terry has to remember is that his name is 'Gerry Blair' and not Terry Shenley."

"He is a very sensible boy," Kyla said, "and also very afraid of what will happen to him if Stepmama finds us."

"Of course he is," Nanny answered. "But I promise you that if that wicked woman gets hold of him, it'll be over my dead body."

Kyla gave a little cry of relief.

She bent forward to kiss Nanny on the cheek.

"I knew you would think of something brilliant," she said. "But what about me?"

"That be easy," Nanny answered. "Your name's 'Miss Taylor' and by some misfortune you were not met as you thought you would be when you left the stagecoach."

She put her hand on Kyla's shoulder before she went on,

"I'll be most apologetic, explainin' that the letter you wrote to me tellin' me about your arrival 'on approval', so to speak, as the Nursery Governess has not yet arrived, So that's why you were not welcomed as you should have been."

Kyla clasped her hands together.

"Nanny, you are such a genius. Everybody in The Castle will accept that story and if she makes enquiries as to who we are, no one will tell Stepmama."

"We can only pray that she is hood-winked," Nanny said. "So if the worse comes to the worst, we shall have to hide Terry."

Kyla smiled while asking Nanny,

"In the secret passages you told us about in your last letter?"

"Well, I did think of that," Nanny admitted. "But it'd be best if there was no suspicion from anybody and no awkward questions."

She spoke firmly, as if she was trying to impress what she was saying on Kyla.

"So I will pray. I will pray very hard," Kyla said, "that your plan will succeed and that Stepmama will never find us."

"I'd like to tell that woman what I think of her," Nanny muttered beneath her breath.

Then, as if she thought that it was a mistake to go on talking, she said,

"Now, you do as I tell you, Miss Kyla, and carry your bags, keepin' in the bushes till you reach halfway up the drive."

"Is that anywhere near the Magic Oak?" Kyla asked.

"Now, who's been tellin' you about that?" Nanny asked. "I can't remember puttin' it in any of my letters."

"It was the highwayman we met on our way here," Kyla said. "Terry will want to tell you all about him."

As she said Terry's name, she saw the expression in Nanny's eyes.

She knew that she would fight like a tiger to protect the little boy who had been put into her arms the moment he had been born.

"Now I'm goin' to find the children," Nanny said. "You do as I tell you and there's no hurry. They'll not expect us back in The Castle till it's teatime."

"I will go to collect our bags," Kyla said, "and thank you, thank you, Nanny. I knew you would help us. It has been very frightening all the time we have been coming here."

"Now, just stop worryin'," Nanny said, "and leave everythin' to me. I'll tell Terry who he's to be and make it a secret game for him and Jane to play. They'll both like that."

"Of course they will," Kyla said. "Being with you, Nanny, is like having Papa and Mama to look after us again."

There was a little catch in her throat as she spoke, which Nanny did not miss.

"Now, run along with you," she said. "We won't start crowin' till we know her Ladyship has given up the chase. With God's help, that's what she'll have to do sooner or later."

"Of course," Kyla agreed.

She moved away as Nanny started resolutely to walk through the bushes onto a twisting path.

Kyla collected the bags that they had put down when they first saw Nanny.

She began to walk slowly and very carefully through the shrubs and among the trees that bordered the drive.

She found it quite heavy work to carry both bags and she was glad that she did not have to move very fast.

In any case it was impossible to walk quickly through the undergrowth.

There appeared to be no one about, but she kept carefully out of sight of The Castle.

Finally, when she had walked quite a long way, she thought that she must have reached about halfway down the drive.

Then, on the other side, she saw the Magic Oak that the highwayman had spoken about.

It was indeed a very old tree and the main trunk was split and two or three of the lowest boughs were propped up.

It was obviously a tree that a great number of strange objects had been attached to over the years.

Even peeping at it from across the drive, Kyla could see that there were envelopes that might contain letters. There were also small objects like dolls that might represent people.

She thought that she also saw a trumpet that could have been put there by a boy and there were ribbons and pieces of material that fluttered in the wind.

There was no sign of anything red.

She thought that, if she did need Bill's help, it would be easy for him to notice something so bright amongst all the other objects and some of them were sodden by rain or had fallen to bits through age.

There was still no one in sight.

She carried the bags, as Nanny had told her, down to the edge of the drive.

She put them on the clipped hedge, as she thought that anyone might have done who had come by in a carriage.

She had just finished, when she saw in the distance, with The Castle silhouetted behind them, Nanny and the two children.

It had always been such a very familiar sight, Nanny in her grey gingham gown with her silver buckle at her waist and her cape of the same material over her shoulders.

She had a small black bonnet on her head with the ribbons tied under her chin.

Kyla felt suddenly happy. It was almost as if she herself was now back in the nursery and everything in the world was all right.

Nanny would never allow anything to hurt or upset her.

They came nearer and she could see that Terry was chattering away.

He was no longer the frightened, pale-faced boy who had sat beside her in the hired post-chaises when they had got away from London.

'There is no need for me to be frightened anymore,' she thought to herself.

Then, almost as if the sun had suddenly gone out, she could hear her stepmother's voice saying in a positively hard tone,

'Then that is what we have to do!'

She felt that she was reaching out towards them menacingly like a dark cloud.

She thought that somehow, by some evil magic, she would catch them and destroy them.

Then she would have the money that she wanted so badly for herself.

All the fears that Kyla had tried to repress on the journey with Terry seemed to sweep over her. It was like a flood tide pushing everything before it.

She could not wait any longer for Nanny and the children to reach her.

She began to walk quickly towards them.

It was only by a tremendous effort of control that she prevented herself from running to them.

*

The Earl of Granston rose from the over-scented and over-comfortable bed and started to dress.

Lisette le Blanc, whom he had just left in the bed, did not speak.

She only raised herself a little against the lace-edged pillows to watch him as he put on his evening clothes.

He did so with a swiftness and expertise that had always infuriated his valet.

It was when the Earl began to tie his cravat in an intricate manner in front of the Cupid-decorated mirror that she spoke up,

"You are very handsome, *mon cher.*"

The Earl, for the first time since he had climbed out of bed, turned his face towards her.

"You are very beautiful, Lisette," he said, "as you very well know."

"Must you leave me?" she asked.

"It is nearly dawn," the Earl replied, "and I need some sleep before I have to face a new day."

Lisette le Blanc laughed and it was a very pretty sound.

She was in fact very attractive with her dark hair falling over her white shoulders.

Her large eyes seemed to fill her small face and it was not only her beauty that had made her one of the most famous and sought-after *courtesans* in the whole of Paris.

It was her amusing wit and a *joie-de-vivre* that was infectious.

The Earl finished tying his cravat.

It had been so skilful done that the points of his collar were neatly on his jawbone.

Still in his shirtsleeves, he walked across the room to sit on the side of the bed, looking at Lisette.

"You have enjoyed tonight?" he asked unexpectedly.

"You have made me very happy," Lisette replied, "*et toi?*"

"You are just as you were the first time I met you," the Earl answered, "and you must promise me never to grow any older."

Lisette chuckled.

"What woman would not wish to keep such a promise? But, *mon brave*, don't leave me for too long. When shall I see you again?"

The Earl did not answer and after a moment she said,

"Tomorrow night or rather tonight!"

"I don't know," the Earl answered, "but I will send you a message sometime during the day. Now let me thank you for tonight."

He bent to kiss her hand as he spoke.

At the same time he thrust a large number of banknotes under her pillow.

Then he rose and put on his evening coat.

It fitted, as had originally been decreed by Beau Brummell himself, without a wrinkle.

He walked towards the door.

"Goodnight, Lisette," he said, "and thank you again."

"*Au revoir, mon cher*," she replied, "and make certain that it is *au revoir* and not *adieu*."

The Earl raised his hand and then went from the room, closing the door behind him.

He walked down the stairs and into the narrow hall.

An elderly servant was dozing in a comfortable armchair.

He rose as he woke up and saw the Earl descending and went to the front door and he did not, however, open it too quickly.

He waited expectantly.

He knew he would receive a *pourboire* if the gentleman who was leaving was as satisfied as he ought to be.

He was not disappointed as the Earl put several gold coins into his hand.

As the man murmured his thanks, he went down the. steps into the street.

The stars were beginning to fade one by one overhead and the first faint light of dawn was shimmering behind the trees in the *Champs-Élysées*.

The Earl strode quickly towards the *Place de la Concorde*.

He had only a short way to go to the apartment where he was staying.

It belonged to one of his friends, who had lent it to him before when he had come to Paris for a visit.

He walked across the *Place de la Concorde* with its fountain still playing.

It was then he knew that, however attractive Lisette le Blanc might be, he had in fact wasted his time and a great deal of money in coming to Paris.

He had been with the Duke of Wellington at Cambrai with the Army of Occupation after the War against Napoleon was finally over.

It was then that Paris had become a Mecca for the young Subalterns in the British Army

They counted the days until they could obtain leave to go to Paris as they so wanted to enjoy all the Festivities to be found in the gay and scintellating City.

The French with their usual shrewdness had started to provide these from the moment that hostilities had ceased.

Restaurants and theatres opened and inevitably the *courtesans*, who had been forgotten during the War, returned.

They seemed to be even more alluring, more attractive and more exotic than ever.

To a young Englishman, they were a revelation and a delight that was totally irresistible.

Yet now the Earl told himself that the old magic was no longer there.

It was not the fault of Lisette and those like her.

It was simply because he had grown older and more fastidious.

As he reached the apartment, he told himself that the sooner he returned to England the better.

In the future Paris would not be included in his itinerary.

As he walked up the stairs, where he knew his valet would be waiting, he wondered what he wanted of life.

While he did not like the word, he was unexpectedly disappointed with Paris.

He recalled how exciting it had been to get away from all his Regimental duties after the War had ended.

Paris was a world which was so different from anything that he had ever known before.

He remembered only too well the dinners, the wine and, above all, the women.

They seemed to glow like flares in the darkness and they ignited a flame within him that was irrepressible.

It had all been a magic that was like a Fairy story and had nothing to do with reality.

All the trappings were still there, the food, the wine, the wit, the laughter and the soft exotic body of Lisette herself.

Yet he knew at once that there was something missing.

He undressed without speaking to his valet, who had been with him throughout the War.

He was wondering what was wrong with his Master and why was he not floating on a cloud as he had felt he was in the past?

He turned towards the comfortable bed that was waiting for him before he said,

"Pack up everything in the morning, Jenkins. We are going back to England."

The valet's eyes lit up.

"That's what I thinks your Lordship'd say," he exclaimed. "And far as I'm concerned, my Lord, the quicker the better."

Tired though he was, the Earl was intrigued.

"Why do you say that, Jenkins?" he asked.

"Paris ain't what it used to be, my Lord," Jenkins replied. "And if you asks me, there's nothin' like home."

He opened the door, carrying the Earl's evening clothes over his arm.

"I'll let your Lordship sleep till I has everythin' ready," he said. "I expects you need it."

He grinned and, before the Earl could reply, he had closed the door.

It was an impertinence, the Earl thought, as he got into bed and pulled the sheets over him.

But Jenkins was irrepressible.

He allowed him liberties that no other servant would take.

But then they had fought together side by side at the Battle of Waterloo.

It had created a closeness between man and man which was difficult to understand in civilian life.

The Earl knew without being told that Jenkins would have died for him at any moment if it had been a question of saving his life.

When a cannonball missed them both by a hair's breadth, they had looked at each other and smiled.

There had been no question of Master and valet, but of two men who faced an enemy together and had survived.

'Jenkins is right!' the Earl told himself. 'I will go home and I will not come back to Paris again.'

At the same time, because he was very intelligent, he was asking himself why the magic was no longer there.

Had he really thought it would be?

'What do I want? What am I looking for? What do I hope to find?'

He asked the questions of himself several times before he fell into a deep sleep.

CHAPTER FOUR

It took the Earl four days to reach London.

When he arrived in the afternoon on Thursday, he was thoroughly bored with travelling.

He went to his house in Berkeley Square, where he was received with some surprise by his large staff.

"We didn't know that your Lordship was a-coming back so soon!" the butler exclaimed. "You knows, my Lord, that Mr. Whitchurch is away?"

The Earl frowned.

Mr. Whitchurch was his excellent secretary, who was adept at seeing to everything in the house including his endless invitations.

He would find things difficult without him, but he had to admit in all fairness that he had told Whitchurch that he did not expect to be back for three weeks or a month.

He could understand that the secretary thought that it was a good time to take a holiday.

He walked into his study.

As he had expected, there was a large pile of letters on his desk, including a number of invitations that must have come as soon as he had left for Paris.

He was quite sure that there would be a similar number, if not more, on Whitchurch's desk which had not even been sorted.

The butler, without being told, brought in a bottle of champagne.

But because he had not been expected, it had not been cooled as it should have been. It was, however, standing in a wine cooler.

After taking a few sips, the Earl decided that he would wait until the ice that surrounded the bottle had done its work.

He was wondering what he should do and where he should go for dinner.

He was aware that the chef would not be at all pleased if he dined in at such short notice.

Then, as he looked at the sun shining on the trees in the centre of Berkeley Square, he thought of Lilliecote Castle.

'I will go to the country,' he decided.

He knew that he had made this decision because he had been disappointed in Paris.

He had no desire at the moment to be social and he was certain that there were a dozen different parties taking place that night, which he would be warmly welcomed to.

But it was too much effort to open all these invitations.

Nor would he bother to read the notes which Whitchurch had left for him on his blotter.

He turned from the window and went upstairs to his bedroom.

Jenkins was already there unpacking the trunks that he had brought back from Paris.

"I'll get your Lordship's bath ready in half-a-jiffy" he said. "Will you be goin' out then, my Lord?"

The Earl made up his mind.

"I'll go to White's Club," he replied. "At least there I shall hear the latest news of what is happening in London."

"If you would ask me, my Lord, it'll be much the same as afore we went away," Jenkins muttered.

Two hours later, the Earl, having bathed and put on his evening clothes, drove in his closed carriage to White's Club.

As he had expected, as soon as he entered, he saw a good number of familiar faces.

The one man he really wanted to see detached himself rapidly from the crowd.

It was Charles Sinclair, his closest friend, who he had been at Eton with.

They had also served in the same Regiment at Waterloo and in the Army of Occupation.

Charles Sinclair hurried to the Earl with outstretched hands.

"Rollo. I had no idea you were back," he exclaimed.

"I have only just returned," the Earl said. "What has been happening in my absence?"

Charles Sinclair laughed.

"Quite a lot and, at the same time, nothing," he replied, "except that I have missed you. Tell me about Paris."

They sat down in two comfortable leather armchairs while Charles Sinclair ordered the drinks.

The Earl looked around him with an air of satisfaction and he felt as if he had been away for a very long time.

There was something comforting in being surrounded by men he had known for years and they were as much a part of his life as his possessions.

The Steward hurried away to fetch the drinks and Charles looked enquiringly at the Earl.

"Why are you back so soon?" he asked. "Did anything go wrong?"

"The only thing that was wrong," the Earl replied, "is that I have grown older and more fastidious and more difficult to please."

Charles threw back his head and laughed.

"You are talking as if you were Methuselah!"

"That is how I feel," the Earl answered. "Quite frankly, Charles, it was a mistake to try to move back into the past."

Charles Sinclair looked sympathetic.

"I know exactly what you mean," he said. "I regretted bitterly that, because my mother needed me, I could not come with you. But now I am glad I stayed behind."

"You certainly saved yourself a great deal of money," the Earl remarked grimly.

"It was expensive enough when we were in the Army of Occupation," Charles said. "I expect those greedy little hands dug deeper into your pocket than ever before."

The Earl knew that this was true and he replied almost irritably,

"I don't want to talk about it! Tell me what has been happening here."

"Prinny, now the King, for one, will be so pleased you are back," Charles said. "I dined with him two nights ago.

He ask tenderly after you and was, I think, somewhat annoyed that you had gone to Paris without telling him where you were going."

"He would have prevented me from going at all," the Earl replied, "or would have given me a lot of things to do which would have interrupted my enjoying myself."

Charles laughed.

It was well known that since he was Prince Regent, he always made anyone who was going abroad bring him back some *objets d'art* for his collection at Carlton House.

What was more, he invariably forgot to pay for them.

Therefore to be what the Earl called one of his 'errand boys' proved exceedingly costly.

"Any new charmers?" the Earl asked.

"No one in particular," Charles replied. "Now I think of it, like you, I am becoming more difficult to please."

The Earl did not answer and he went on,

"At one time I thought that each Incomparable was Aphrodite herself. Now I find myself being critical and finding fault with them."

The Earl was smiling and his eyes were twinkling as he said,

"You mean their necks are too long or too short, their noses turn up instead of down and their hair is not silken to the touch as it was when we first found women irresistible."

Charles clapped his hands.

"Rollo, you are becoming a poet! It is exactly what I was feeling and could not put into words!"

They sat laughing and drinking until Charles suggested,

"Why do we not have some dinner here and then go on to one of the balls taking place tonight? I promised to look in at the Duchess of Bedford's. I know she will be thrilled to see you."

"I expect her invitation will be somewhere on my desk in Berkeley Square," the Earl answered. "Doubtless Whitchurch has said that I am away and will have refused it."

"Which means the Duchess will be all the more delighted to see you," Charles said. "Do not forget, Rollo, that you are a very eligible bachelor and all the pushy Mamas sitting on the dais get excited the moment you come in sight."

"Oh, shut up!" the Earl exclaimed. "As you well know, you are just as eligible as I am."

"Nonsense!" Charles replied. "I am only the son of a Viscount. As my father is hale and hearty at just over fifty, it will be half a century before they see me in the House of Lords!"

"Where doubtless, unless you are then blind and deaf, you will enjoy hearing the sound of your own voice," the Earl retorted.

Laughing and teasing each other, they walked up the stairs to the dining room.

They could have easily joined a number of other friends at other tables.

Instead they chose a table to themselves and by the time that they had finished dinner, the Earl was in a good humour.

He knew that he had enjoyed the evening so much more than he had enjoyed himself in Paris.

They drove to the Duke of Bedford's large and imposing house in Islington Square.

They found, as the Earl had expected, that the dance floor was very crowded and almost everyone of any social consequence was present.

The Duke and Duchess greeted him enthusiastically.

Almost immediately he was surrounded by a number of attractive women, welcoming him back as if he had been on a trip to the moon.

"How could you desert us?" one lovely Marchioness asked. "What is worse, you never said 'goodbye' to me."

There was a very reproachful note in her voice and the only thing that the Earl could do was to apologise profusely.

"I will forgive you," the Marchioness said, "only if you will call on me tomorrow. I shall be waiting for you at four o'clock."

Her eyes searched his for a response to the invitation on her pouting lips.

There was just a little pause before the Earl exclaimed,

"I will certainly come if I am in London, but I may have to go to the country."

"You are being evasive," she complained. "I cannot understand why."

She would have said more, but at that very moment her partner claimed her for the next dance.

She was obliged to move away, giving a backward glance over her shoulder at the Earl as she did so.

He looked round and saw an alluring lady who he had had a brief *affaire de coeur* with.

She had a complaisant husband who turned a blind eye to her love affairs and spent his time in the country breeding thoroughbreds.

But before the Earl could move in her direction, a very smartly dressed woman, whom he did not know, came up to him.

"We have never been introduced, my Lord," she said, "but my name is Lady Shenley and I have heard so much about your magnificent and beautiful Castle."

"I am, indeed very proud of it," the Earl responded.

"That is not surprising," Lady Shenley replied. "I have a special interest in it because the Nanny who was devoted to my two stepchildren is now looking after a child who I believe is your niece."

"Yes, that is so," the Earl said. "My niece, Jane, is living with me while my brother-in-law is Governor of Aden. He and my sister thought that the heat there would be too much for her."

"How sensible," Lady Shenley exclaimed. "I would love to see dear old Nanny again. I wonder if, as I expect to be, I am in the vicinity of your Castle next week, I might call on her."

"As I shall be in The Castle myself," the Earl said, "I will be delighted to welcome you in person."

"How very kind, my Lord, and I am longing to see your Castle."

"Then, of course, I will show it to you," the Earl affirmed.

"I will reach Lilliecote by Sunday if that is not too soon?" Lady Shenley asked.

"I am thinking of going home tomorrow," the Earl answered. "So I shall look forward to your visit."

"You are kindness itself," Lady Shenley said. "Thank you very very much."

She spoke in such a heartfelt tone that he was really rather touched.

Then, when he would have spoken to her again, he felt a touch on his arm.

An elderly woman was beside him, who he saw was the Duchess of Northumberland.

She had been a friend of his mother's and he exclaimed,

"How delightful to see you, Your Grace. I did not know that you were in London."

"My granddaughter is making her debut this Season," the Duchess replied, "and so I am chaperoning her here tonight. How are you, Rollo? But I need not ask you this question. I have never seen you looking better."

"And I can say the same of you," the Earl answered gallantly.

He knew that the Duchess was over seventy and he thought that it was very sporting of her to come to London to chaperone her grandchild.

The Duchess drew him a little to one side and they could talk more comfortably against an open window.

"I saw that tiresome woman, Lady Shenley, speaking to you," she then said.

"Tiresome?" the Earl enquired.

"She is very pushing and I consider it disgraceful that she should appear at a party like this so soon after her husband's death. He was such a charming man."

The Earl gave an exclamation.

"Now I know who you are talking about. I knew Lord Shenley and always thought him, as you say, charming and very intelligent. I did hear that he had married again after his wife died, but did not expect anyone so young."

He was about to add the word *glamorous*, but thought that it might somehow offend the Duchess.

"I have no wish to talk to you about that woman," the Duchess said sharply, "but about The Castle. Is the garden still as beautiful as your mother made it?"

"You know that I would not fail her in that respect," the Earl answered. "She adored the garden and someone said only last month that it was the best-laid-out garden in the whole of England."

The Duchess sighed.

"That is exactly what your mother would have liked to hear. Although I have tried to copy her in my own garden, I am afraid that it is a very difficult thing to do."

They talked for a little while longer and then the Duchess, remembering why she was at the ball in the first place, insisted on introducing the Earl to her granddaughter.

As he might have expected, the girl was rather gauche, shy and not particularly pretty.

However, he did his duty by dancing with her.

When it was over, he returned her to her grandmother's side.

"I shall be giving a dance for Imogen next month," the Duchess said, "and I shall be very hurt, Rollo, if you do not attend it, even though I know you are longing to tell me that you are not particularly interested in *debutantes*."

As the remark was unexpected, the Earl laughed.

"Your Grace is taking the very words out of my mouth."

"I knew that was what you were thinking," the Duchess said shrewdly. "I promise you there will also be a great many of your special friends present and do not forget that, however alluring they may be now, they started their social lives as *debutantes*."

The Earl could only laugh again.

However, he promised the Duchess that he really would come to her party.

Then he went in search of one of his friends who, as the Duchess had said, were all very alluring.

He found her and finally led her towards the garden.

As he did so, he was aware that Lady Shenley was watching him.

He remembered what the Duchess said about her and, at the same time, he thought it was a little unkind.

She was obviously much younger than her husband, Lord Shenley, had been.

It seemed rather hard that she should be reproved for attending parties.

He calculated that it must be over six months now since she went into mourning.

'Older people' he thought, 'like to weep and wail dramatically for a very long time. 'For younger women it could only be tedious and a waste of their youth.'

*

He did not stay very late at the ball.

Charles was obviously enjoying himself and had no wish to leave,

The Earl drove back alone in his carriage to Berkeley Square.

As he climbed into bed, he gave Jenkins instructions that they would leave tomorrow for The Castle.

He would drive a new team of chestnuts, which he had only recently bought.

They were, without exception, the best matched horses in the whole of the *Beau Ton*.

*

Kyla and Terry were completely entranced by The Castle.

After what Nanny had written to them, they had expected it to be large and impressive.

But what was very exciting was that everything was not only historical but so tastefully arranged that every room was a picture in itself.

The Castle had been added to by almost every generation.

There were many closets with diamond-paned windows and huge rooms with very large windows, magnificent marble fireplaces and painted ceilings.

Nanny took them round herself.

While she knew a little of the history, Kyla longed to know more.

"There's no Curator at the moment," Nanny explained, "because the man who's been here for years has been taken ill. But I thinks you'll find a lot of interestin' books in the library and perhaps a catalogue which'll tell you all you want to know."

The library itself was magnificent and Nanny said it contained over ten thousand books.

The balcony, for access to the upper shelves, was reached by a spiral brass staircase.

"And now show us the secret passages," Terry begged her.

"I think that his Lordship ought to do that," Nanny replied. "They wouldn't be secret if everyone knew about them."

"But you have found out where they are, have you not, Nanny?"

Kyla was smiling as she spoke.

She knew that Nanny was always curious and would find it impossible not to try to discover anything that might be hidden from her.

"I'm not goin' to say that I've no idea where they are," Nanny replied.

"Please show us just one, please," Terry pleaded.

Nanny looked over her shoulder to make sure that no one was listening.

But, as the Earl was not at home, there was only one footman on duty in case someone called unexpectedly.

The servants kept to their own quarters and now they were relaxing in the housekeeper's room, the pantry and the big servants' hall, which was opposite the kitchen.

"Very well, I'll show you one" Nanny said, making up her mind. "But you're *not* to tell his Lordship what I've done and you are not to talk about it to any of the other staff. Do you understand?"

"It's a secret," Terry said, "and I promise I will keep it a secret."

"Then come with me," Nanny proposed.

She touched a secret catch in the panelling at the back of the library.

It opened slowly and Terry gave a gasp of excitement.

"Can we go in? Please, Nanny, can we go in?"

"Yes, we'll go in," Nanny said. "And I'll show you how this passage takes us right up to the nursery floor."

She closed the panelling behind them as she spoke.

Kyla realised, very much to her surprise, that the secret passage was lit in an exceedingly clever way.

There was not more than a dim light, but just enough to show the way and it came from some openings in the construction of the walls.

Nanny said that it had been done at the time when Cromwellian Troops were hunting the Royalists in the Civil War.

"Other passages," she continued, "were made earlier than this when Queen Mary was persecuting the Protestants and later her sister, Queen Elizabeth, the Roman Catholics."

Kyla looked at her admiringly.

"How clever of you to know all this, Nanny."

"Well, I couldn't live in The Castle and not learn a little about it," Nanny replied. "So I makes friends with the Curator and, as he seldom has anyone to talk to, he tells me what I wants to know."

"And that is very very exciting for us," Terry enthused.

He began to walk ahead of them along the narrow passage.

After a short way there were some steps leading up to the next floor and a little further on they came to what Nanny told them was a Priest's Hole.

It was actually a small room with an Altar on one of the walls and a wooden bedstead on another.

"So this is where the Priests hid?" Kyla said.

"That's right," Nanny agreed. "The Curator told me that the family used to creep in here to hear Mass while the

Priest himself did not dare to go out for fear that he should be seen, arrested and beheaded."

Kyla gave a little cry.

"They were very cruel in those days!"

As she spoke, she thought that the same might be said for today.

Could anything be crueller than her stepmother plans to kill dear Terry? And to sell her into a life of debauchery, which she would rather die than endure?

Nanny did not say anything, but Kyla knew that she was thinking the same thing.

To change the subject, Nanny suggested,

"Now, come along and I'll show you how you can reach the nursery without goin' back to the front of the house."

They walked a long way along another dimly lit passage.

Finally at the far end of it there was a ladder attached to the wall.

Nanny climbed up it first and at the top she pushed open a trap door.

Kyla followed behind her.

She found that they were now in a large cupboard that was obviously used for things that were not wanted and for luggage, like their own, which was too small to be taken up to the attics.

Terry joined them in the cupboard and Nanny pulled the trap door back into place.

Unless anyone looked very carefully it would not be noticed and so no one would have suspected for a moment that an entrance to a secret passage was there in front of them.

In fact, to make sure it was not observed, there was a rug covering it.

Made of light wool, it was not heavy enough to prevent anyone from pushing open the trap from below.

Terry was really delighted with everything he had seen.

"Now I can creep about The Castle," he asserted, "and no one will know that I am there."

Nanny and Kyla exchanged glances.

They were both thinking that if the worse came to the worst and their stepmother came in search of them, this was where they could hide.

"Now just you forget all you've seen," Nanny ordered, "or you will get me into trouble. You promise, Terry, not to talk about it?"

"Of course, I promise," Terry answered.

Nanny opened the cupboard door and they found that they were in another passage at the other end of which was the nursery.

Jane had been lying down while they were exploring The Castle because she was rather tired.

She was awake now and the nursery maid was putting her into one of her pretty frilly dresses.

"You are back," she said excitedly. "I was afraid you would forget about me."

"We haven't done that," Nanny answered. "And I have asked the chef to send you up somethin' special for tea, somethin' I know that both you and Terry will like."

"Chocolate cake!" Jane exclaimed.

"Wait and see," Nanny retorted.

But Kyla knew that Nanny had not forgotten that chocolate cake was Terry's favourite.

After tea they played games and then first Jane went to bed and an hour later Terry.

After that Kyla sat and talked with Nanny in the nursery.

"Have you thought," she asked Nanny, "what we shall do when the Earl comes back? After all he cannot expect to keep Lady Blessingham's grandson for ever."

"I know," Nanny said in a worried voice. "At the same time it's a mistake to look too far ahead. His Lordship, bein' a young man, is not particularly interested in children."

"Surely he likes Jane, who is such a pretty child?" Kyla enquired.

"Oh, he's very kind to her and begrudges her nothin', which is very much for her good," Nanny said. "But I think actually it's time now he was thinkin' of gettin' married and havin' children of his own."

"He has gone to Paris," Kyla said. "I heard my stepmother say it was a City of gaiety and every possible excitement for men, so he will not be thinking of choosing a wife as yet."

"No real lady would talk about such things in front of you anyway," Nanny said stiffly.

"I think Stepmama was envious that any man preferred going to Paris to being in London with her," Kyla said. "Of course she was not talking to me but to her friends, who said some very strange things that I did not understand."

"A very good thing too, if you asks me," Nanny said tartly. "I never did think that her Ladyship was in any way a good companion for a young and innocent girl."

Actually, because she was intelligent, Kyla had thought that herself.

She did not want to think about her stepmother let alone talk about her, so she said,

"What worries me, Nanny is how we can get hold of any money. When what I have now is spent and I have sold Mama's jewels, there will be no question of our having any more. Unless, of course, we no longer remain in hiding and reveal who we are to Papa's Bank or to his Solicitors."

"You can't do that," Nanny stressed.

"I know," Kyla answered. 'That is what worries me. And, as you well know, Terry must go to school sometime."

Nanny held up her hands.

"We can't talk now about Terry goin' to school or you two livin' on your own. We shall just have to wait and see what happens. In the meantime you're ever so safe here with me."

"It is wonderful of you to have us," Kyla said. "I thank God that we are here with you and are not wandering about the country being frightened by highwaymen."

"Terry has told me all about that man, Bill, who was kind to you," Nanny remarked.

"I was so sorry for him," Kyla said, "because really he is just one of the people whose lives were ruined by that horrible War."

Nanny nodded.

"Wars are bad and wicked. Mr. Jenkins, that's his Lordship's valet, had said more than once it was a miracle that he and his Lordship survived and were not killed by that monster, Napoleon."

"So perhaps it is easier to fight an enemy in a war than to be like us" Kyla said in a low tone, "not knowing who is our friend and who is our enemy."

"There be no mistakin' who *your* enemy is," Nanny said sharply. "'Tis her Ladyship and if there is any justice in this world, she'll surely get her just deserts."

"In the meantime we are fugitives," Kyla said. "When I think of the long years ahead for us, hiding or running away, it frightens me so much."

Nanny pressed her lips together.

Kyla knew that she was preventing herself from denouncing her stepmother as well.

After a few seconds, Nanny suggested,

"Stop worryin', Miss Kyla. Just go to bed and thank God that you have somewhere to sleep, that you're not hungry and now there's no danger or I should know about it."

Kyla rose from her chair, saying,

"You are right, Nanny. I am being selfish and ungrateful in thinking about myself and Terry when you are doing so much for us."

"You're nothin' of the kind," Nanny contradicted her. "You're just tired and, when one's tired, things always seem worse."

"I know that," Kyla said. "At the same time I feel as if Stepmama is coming nearer and nearer to us. You will think it is silly of me, Nanny, but I feel that she will never give up until she has found us. And, of course, sooner or later she will come to see you."

"When that happens, I'll deal with it," Nanny said. "Now, dear, go to bed and remember, if nothin' else, your father and your mother are lookin' after you."

Kyla smiled.

"Of course they are. You always say the right thing, Nanny."

She kissed her and then went to the small bedroom, which was only a little way down the passage.

The room next to Nanny's, which was used when there were two children in the nursery, was occupied by Terry and she knew that Nanny would watch over him just like a Guardian Angel.

Whatever happened in the night, he would be safe with her.

When Kyla reached her own room, she went to the window to look out.

The moon was shining vividly on the trees in the Park and on the lake that lay just below the house.

It was so beautiful and at the same time so spiritual that it seemed impossible that there was any real evil. An evil that wanted to destroy Terry and herself.

Kyla looked up to the stars.

'Help us, help us,' she murmured in her heart.

She felt, as they twinkled back, that they had received her message and that she need not be afraid.

When she climbed into bed, it was a long time before she could fall asleep.

*

The following day the sun was shining brightly.

Nanny thought it would amuse Jane and Terry if they took a picnic up to the wood and the tree house.

It really was a very tiny house, which had been built not for Jane but for her uncle when he was a small boy.

It was a very skilful piece of carpentry. There were eight steps up into the house, which was suspended between four trees that grew close together.

It was built of timber itself, split down the centre and used both for the roof, the walls and the floor and it was big enough to hold Terry and Jane together comfortably.

Nanny and Kyla sat outside on the sandy ground and spread out the picnic.

From the tree house the children could see over the bushes and catch a glimpse of The Castle.

"We can see if anyone approaches us," Terry said. "And if they are enemies, we could shoot them down."

"We would have to be careful," Jane replied, "in case we shot a friend. How would we know who was an enemy unless he was waving a sword or a gun at us?"

"If it was a war, he would be a soldier and wearing a uniform," Terry said. "If he was in a French uniform, then we would know that he was our enemy."

"Not today," Kyla interjected. "Now that the War is well and truly over, we are friendly with the French and they are no longer our enemies."

"That be true enough," Nanny said, "but I wouldn't trust them far. I only hopes that his Lordship doesn't get into trouble goin' off to Paris as he has."

"I would love to go to Paris," Kyla said. "In fact I would like to go anywhere abroad. I have read about other countries in books but that is not the same as visiting them."

"You'll have to wait until you are married," Nanny said, "and then your husband'll take you. Let's, hope he be rich enough to have a private yacht, as I hear some of them ships that cross the Channel are uncomfortable and not particularly safe."

Kyla was about to reply that she thought it unlikely that she would ever get married.

How would she ever meet a man when she was in hiding?

And if she did by any chance meet one, it would be impossible to be married without the permission of her Guardian, who was her stepmother.

'It is no use' she thought to herself, 'worrying about the future. Nanny is right, we just have to take things day by day.'

At the same time, it was frightening to think that they might have to go on like this for years and years.

She would be hiding with Terry without money and without friends.

And certainly, where she was concerned, without marriage.

Terry and Jane were laughing happily together.

They had carried their food up into the house and sat cross-legged on the floor to eat it.

"Chocolate cake and iced biscuits," Terry cried. "I have a cherry on mine."

"I have two cherries on mine," Jane said, having no wish to be outdone.

'He is happy,' Kyla told herself. 'There is no reason for him to fear the future with both Nanny and me looking after him.'

When tea was over, they packed up and went back to The Castle.

They played card games in the nursery until it was time for Jane to go to bed.

"I don't want to leave Terry," she protested painfully.

"I'll tell you just what you can do," Nanny said. "Have your bath and change into your nightgown and then we can all have supper together as a special treat."

Jane jumped for joy at this suggestion.

Betty, the nursery maid, who was a girl of only sixteen, helped Nanny give Jane her bath.

She then cleared everything up and Jane joined Terry and Kyla in the nursery.

Kyla had also changed from the dress she had worn all day into one that was made of muslin.

She had put it in her bag because it was light and easy to carry.

It was, in fact, a very pretty gown, which she had bought to wear at home when there were no guests. And it made her look very young.

She brushed her hair and the last rays of the sun coming through the window turned her curls into shining gold with a touch of flame in them.

Nanny had had a talk with the chef and besides a well-cooked fish for their supper he had provided a special dish of strawberries, cream and meringues.

The dessert was in the shape of a boat and not only Jane but Terry too was delighted with it and the two children nearly ate the whole dish.

"It was very clever of the chef, wasn't it?" Terry asked Kyla.

"Very clever," she answered. "And I know that he would be pleased if you sent him a message to say how much you enjoyed it."

"I will," Terry nodded. "Perhaps tomorrow he will make us another exciting pudding."

Kyla was teasing him for being greedy and they were all laughing when suddenly the door opened.

A man came into the nursery.

As Nanny rose quickly to her feet, Kyla realised that he must be *the Earl*.

He was looking exceedingly smart and, when he saw who was at the table, he looked surprised.

"Good evening, Nanny," he began.

Nanny curtseyed.

"Good evening, my Lord. We were not expectin' you back so soon."

"That is what everyone has said to me," the Earl replied. "And I am beginning to feel that there is something reproachful in the way they say it."

"Oh, no, of course not," Nanny said. "I'm sure everybody is delighted that your Lordship is back."

"I see you are having a party," the Earl commented.

"While your Lordship was away, Lady Blessingham, who your Lordship'll remember recommended me when I applied for the position, came to see me, bringin' her grandson, Gerald Blair. She was going to ask your Lordship if you could have him to stay for a few days while she is visiting her sister, who has been taken ill."

"Of course you said that I would be delighted to do so," the Earl said.

He was walking round the table as he was speaking and he bent down to kiss Jane.

"What have you been doing while I have been away?" he asked her.

"Playing in my tree house, Uncle Rollo," Jane replied. "G-Gerry finds it very exciting."

The Earl held out his hand to Terry.

"I hope you also like my Castle," he said.

"It's absolutely spiffing," Terry replied. "The biggest Castle I have ever seen."

Now the Earl looked at Kyla and he was obviously surprised at her appearance.

"This is Miss Taylor," Nanny said quickly. "Mr. Whitchurch by now will have told your Lordship that I suggested that Jane should have a nursery Governess now that she has passed seven, to teach her. Miss Taylor be here on approval."

Kyla curtseyed and the Earl said,

"You look very young to be a Governess."

"I hope, my Lord," Kyla replied, "I am old enough to be able to teach Jane all she needs to know."

"We shall have to discuss that," the Earl responded.

He looked at Nanny.

"I am glad you are all right. I will write to my sister and tell her that Jane is very happy, and has someone to play with. I have always felt that it was important."

"I agree with your Lordship," Nanny said, "and then Jane will be writin' to her mother tomorrow as she does every week."

"Quite right," the Earl replied.

He walked towards the door.

As he reached it, he looked back.

"I will talk to Miss Taylor tomorrow," he said. "In the meantime I am sure that Jane and her young friend would like to ride with me tomorrow morning."

"I want to do that," Terry said before anyone could speak. "I am sure your horses are magnificent, but Nanny would not let me ride one without your permission."

"I am giving it to you now," the Earl answered, "and I hope you are indeed a good rider."

"I am good. Very good, aren't I, Kyla?"

He spoke impulsively and Kyla realised too late that Nanny had not chosen a Christian name for her.

She had, however, made it clear to Terry that he must pretend they had not met before they had come to The Castle.

Because she was aware of the mistake, Nanny said rapidly,

"Lady Blessingham told me and Miss Taylor when she arrived that her grandson was a very good rider. I don't think your Lordship need be afraid that he'll injure one of your horses or himself."

"That is certainly reassuring," the Earl replied.

He went from the nursery and closed the door behind him.

As he walked downstairs, he was aware that something was rather puzzling.

Miss Taylor was frightened. He had seen the fear in her eyes.

He had a suspicion, although it seemed absurd, that, when he spoke to her, she trembled.

The Earl had been a very astute Officer during the War against Napoleon.

In fact the Duke of Wellington had used him to interrogate the prisoners they captured.

Also, he was in charge of Intelligence where it concerned his own Regiment. So he was well used to scrutinising people.

He used his instincts where they were concerned rather than trusting to what they said.

He walked down the main staircase and into the hall.

His instinct told him that there was something out of the ordinary about Miss Taylor, something that he was determined to find out about before he formally engaged her.

CHAPTER FIVE

The Earl dined alone.

The chef provided an excellent dinner considering that he had not been expected.

Before he left London, the Earl had sent a note to his friend Charles Sinclair asking him to join him as soon as he possibly could.

He guessed that he would have quite a number of engagements that he would not want to chuck at the last moment.

At the same time he was very certain that Charles would not fail him.

When he rose from the table to go towards the study, he suddenly thought that it would be a good idea to see Miss Taylor now.

It was still quite early and she would not have gone to bed.

He was eager to know a lot more about her and also to discover, if possible, why she was frightened.

He therefore said to the butler,

"Ask Miss Taylor to come to me in the study."

"Very good, my Lord," the man replied.

A footman hurried to open the door and the Earl left the dining room.

In his study he looked once again at the large amount of correspondence on his desk and he then decided that he had no intention of coping with it until Whitchurch returned.

The secretary did have an assistant who would help in dealing with the many farmers and tenants on the estate. But the Earl thought that it would be a mistake if his letters were looked at by anyone but his private secretary.

He was pleased to see that since his arrival, flowers had been brought into the study and also the windows had been opened.

He thought with satisfaction that The Castle was run almost with complete perfection and he was proud that things had not deteriorated in any way since his mother had died.

He picked up one of the newspapers that he had brought with him from London and he was reading the editorial in *The Times* when the door opened.

"Miss Taylor, my Lord," the butler announced.

The Earl looked up and saw Kyla standing just inside the study.

He appreciated the simple gown that she was wearing, which made her look very young.

At the same time he was aware, because he was extremely perceptive, that it was by no means a cheap garment.

It must, he thought, have cost more than anyone earning on the wages of a Governess could afford.

"I have thought, Miss Taylor," he said, "that, as I may have company with me tomorrow evening, we should have our talk now about what you intend to teach my niece."

He indicated a chair and added,

"Suppose you sit down."

Kyla walked to the chair with a grace that the Earl knew was not assumed.

She seated herself on the edge of the chair and put her hands in her lap.

She looked just like a child who was about to receive instructions from an adult.

"Now, suppose we start at the beginning," the Earl said. "As my secretary is not here to tell me anything about you, tell me about yourself."

As he spoke, he was fully aware that the fear was back in Miss Taylor's eyes.

And she was quite obviously nervous of answering his request.

There was a long pause before finally she said,

"I had heard that a Governess was – needed here at The Castle and so I – came for an – interview. The letter I wrote announcing the time – of my arrival was – lost in the post."

"So what happened?" the Earl asked.

"I walked from the – stagecoach stop and met Nanny and the – little boy in the drive."

"You had not met my niece's Nanny before?"

There was another pause before Kyla answered in a low voice,

"N-no."

"And where did you come from?" the Earl enquired.

"I came from – London."

There was no doubt that the words seemed to be dragged from Miss Taylor's lips.

"Were you working in London as a Governess?" the Earl next asked.

"No, my Lord. I was – staying with friends."

"I thought perhaps you lived in London," the Earl said. "Where is your home?"

He had no doubt as he watched her that Miss Taylor was having difficulty in answering his questions.

Now, after a moment, she replied,

"My home is in the – country. As my parents are – dead, I have to – find work where there is also – accommodation for me."

"I understand," the Earl said, "and, of course, you consider yourself capable of teaching children because you yourself have had a good education."

"Yes, a very good one," she said quickly, "and I speak French and German, although, of course, Lady Jane is too young to learn languages yet."

"You say that your parents are dead," the Earl said after a pause. "What did your father do?"

He realised at once that this was another difficult question for Miss Taylor to answer.

She hesitated quite obviously before she replied,

"He had some land and he was very knowledgeable – about horses."

"In consequence," the Earl said, "I suppose you are a good rider?"

For the first time Miss Taylor smiled.

"I hope so, I have ridden almost since I left the cradle."

The Earl laughed.

Then he said,

"That will be useful, at any rate, when I am not here. I want my niece to ride every day and it would be better for her to be accompanied by her Governess than just a groom."

Now Miss Taylor raised her head.

He saw that the fear had gone from her eyes and she was looking interested.

"Is your Lordship saying that I can ride – your horses?" she asked.

"If you can hold them," the Earl replied. "I will see for myself if you are competent to do that. You had better come riding with the children tomorrow morning."

"Oh, thank you, thank you!"

There was no doubt that Miss Taylor was pleased at the idea.

To the Earl's surprise she rose to her feet.

"I hope," she then said in a low voice, "that I will not disappoint your Lordship either as a rider or a teacher, as I want very much to stay on in this beautiful Castle."

She curtseyed and, without waiting for the Earl to say anything, she went to the door.

For a moment he contemplated calling her back to say that he had not finished with her.

Then, because he knew that it would upset her, he said nothing.

Instead he just watched her open the door and leave the room.

Only when she had gone did he tell himself that she was even more unusual than he had expected.

There was no doubt too that, while she was frightened of him, it was not just because he was her employer or of great Social standing.

He was not certain how he knew it, but he was sure that it was something deeper.

It was something that he could not diagnose and yet he knew that it was there.

Anything mysterious and unusual always intrigued the Earl.

He had, in fact, although he would not admit it, missed the Intelligence work that he had done during the War.

Now he found himself thinking of Miss Taylor until he went up to bed.

'There is definitely some mystery here,' he mused.

And he was determined to get to the bottom of it.

*

The next morning was Sunday.

As Nanny explained to Kyla, they did not go to Morning Service in the village Church.

The Chaplain would come to The Castle at six o'clock in the evening to hold a special Service for all the household in the Earl's Private Chapel.

"I have not seen the Private Chapel yet" Kyla said.

"It's very impressive," Nanny replied, "and was built in the reign of King Henry VIII. Of course it's been added to since with stained glass windows and fine pictures. But everyone who comes here says it's different from every other Chapel they have ever seen."

"Then you know that I will look forward to seeing it," Kyla said. "There is lots more too that I want to see of The Castle itself."

"I'll show it to you as soon as his Lordship goes away again," Nanny promised.

She had asked Kyla when she had returned to the nursery last night what had happened.

She was relieved that the questions were no more difficult nor, she hoped, likely to make the Earl suspicious.

"What worries me," Kyla had said, "is how we will explain to his Lordship that Terry is staying here for so long."

"I'll think of somethin'," Nanny said firmly. "As I've said before, dearie, it be no use anticipatin' what'll happen in the future. We'll just have to wait and see."

"I am quite content with that as long as I can wait and see it all with you, Nanny," Kyla replied.

She kissed her affectionately goodnight.

*

When she awoke, she suddenly realised that, while the Earl had invited her to ride with them, she did not have a habit with her.

As it was heavy, it was the first thing that she had decided not to include in her luggage.

She ran into the nursery before breakfast to say to Nanny,

"What can I do? His Lordship said last night that I could ride with him and the children. I never thought to bring a habit with me."

Nanny thought for a moment and then she proposed,

"I don't think there'll be any difficulty about that. I've been told over and over again that the housekeeper, Mrs. Field, is a real hoarder and has kept all the clothes that Jane's mother wore ever since she was a child."

"Do you really think she will have a habit I could borrow?"

"Just leave it to me," Nanny smiled.

She went from the nursery and, when she came back, Kyla gave a cry of joy.

Nanny was carrying three habits over her arm.

She held them out and Kyla was very sure that one of them would fit her.

"Her Ladyship wore these when she was younger than you," Nanny explained. "Mrs. Field told me that she has grown much fatter in the last few years and so she'll never wear them again."

"I love this one," Kyla exclaimed.

She picked out a habit that was a deep blue in colour and made in a soft material.

"Try it on," Nanny said. "Now, hurry! His Lordship'll be angry if any of you are late."

Kyla was not late and Mrs. Field provided her with a riding hat and boots as well.

She had some trouble in finding her boots of the right size.

"Your feet, Miss Taylor, are smaller than her Ladyship's," she said. "In fact the pair of boots that you're wearin' now she wore when she was eleven."

"Then I must be very careful with them," Kyla replied with a smile, "because Lady Jane will be wanting them soon."

Mrs. Field gave a toss of her head.

"There's no need for her Ladyship to have anythin' but what's new and the best. His Lordship's a rich man."

"Then everyone here is very lucky," Kyla exclaimed.

She was speaking more to herself than to the housekeeper.

She was thinking that it was lack of money that was at the bottom of all their troubles.

If her father had been rich enough to leave her stepmother everything she required, she would not be intending to murder Terry and dispose of her.

Then Kyla told herself that it was really silly of her to think about such things.

It was a lovely day and the sun was shining brightly in the sky.

She was going to ride one of the Earl's superlative horses that she had admired when she had seen them in the paddock and she had learnt from Nanny that the Earl was acknowledged to have the finest stable in the County.

Mrs. Field also provided Terry with a pair of riding boots and Lady Jane looked sweet in a pale blue habit that matched her eyes and her little bonnet had ribbons which tied under her chin.

As the children were so excited, when it was time to go downstairs, they ran ahead.

Kyla could only hope that Terry would not forget that his name was 'Gerald Blair' and that he must not address her as 'Kyla'.

She was sure that it was something he would not do again and he had indeed been very punctilious yesterday in addressing her as 'Miss Taylor' as she had told him to do.

When they reached the stables, the horses that the Earl had ordered had just been brought out of the stalls.

There was a pony for Jane and a horse that was not too large for Terry.

The next horse was so magnificent that Kyla was quite certain that it was not meant for her.

Then, as she was looking at it appreciatively, she heard a voice behind her say,

"Do you think you can manage Firefly?"

Kyla turned her head.

"Do you really mean it, my Lord," she asked, "that I can ride anything so magnificent? Thank you! *Thank you!*"

"I thought it would please you," the Earl answered.

There was a fine black stallion for him that was the equal of if not superior to Firefly.

When they set off from the stable, the Earl rode ahead with the children on one side of him.

Kyla thought it a pity that there was no famous artist there to paint a picture of them.

The Earl took them first to the paddock.

"I want you to ride round," he said. "In fact you can race if you like. I want to see just how well you all ride."

"You have seen me before, Uncle Rollo," Jane pointed out.

The Earl smiled at her.

"I know and you are a very good rider just like your mother."

"And you," Jane answered.

"Let me see if you can beat the other two riders," the Earl suggested.

Quickly and with an expertise that made Kyla realise that he had done it before, he put them on different starting points.

It gave even Jane a chance of winning the race.

Then, when he gave the word, they all set off.

Kyla naturally began a long way behind Terry and she realised as soon as she handled Firefly that he was one of the finest horses that she had ever ridden.

He responded to her touch and, when she talked to him, she felt that he understood every word.

She told herself that it would be a mistake to try to rush ahead and pass the children.

She therefore deliberately drew Firefly in and then they all rode twice round the paddock together and ended up in front of the Earl.

Terry won, Jane was a close second and Kyla, still holding Firefly back, was third.

She knew as she rode up to the Earl that he realised what she had been doing.

"Well, Miss Taylor," he asked, "what is your verdict?"

"I thought we were waiting for yours, my Lord."

"You know without my telling you that you are an outstanding rider," he said. "In fact, exceptional. I wondered if you would manage to hold in Firefly or would have to surge ahead as he wished to do."

Kyla did not answer the Earl.

She merely smiled and he added,

"One day I will race you and it will be interesting to see which of us wins."

"I am quite certain, my Lord, that would be a foregone conclusion," Kyla replied. "But it is something I should greatly enjoy."

Looking at the children the Earl said,

"Now we are going for a ride on the flat land and you, Jane and Gerald can see how fast you can make your horses go."

They were both delighted at this idea.

As they rushed ahead, the Earl and Kyla came more slowly behind them.

"Were your father's horses as fine as Firefly?" the Earl asked.

"You know the answer to that question, my Lord," Kyla replied. "I don't suppose there are more than one or two owners in the whole of England who have horses as fine as Firefly and your stallion."

"That is what I like to think myself. I have spent a great deal of time breeding horses as well as buying them and I want you to see my brood mares."

"I would love to," Kyla exclaimed. "Have you bred any Arabians?"

"Now it is most strange that you should ask," the Earl remarked, "because I know it is something that my stables lack. I intend to go out to Syria this winter to see what is on offer."

"How exciting," Kyla said. "That will be a wonderful experience – for you."

She spoke wistfully.

The Earl then found that he could read her thoughts and knew that it was something she longed to do herself.

He thought it odd as most women of his acquaintance would find it incredibly boring to spend a lot of time looking at horses. They would much prefer talking to him and, of course, making love.

It flashed through his mind that it would be rather amusing to take someone so young and unspoiled with him to Syria.

Then he told himself sharply that it was not the sort of thing he should be thinking about a Governess who he might employ.

He had never concerned himself with his own servants or with anyone else's.

Quickly he told the children that now they were to ride each side of him.

Miss Taylor could therefore ride behind.

Kyla realised as he spoke that something had annoyed him and wondered what it could be.

She also had the idea that in telling her to ride behind, he was putting her in her rightful place.

He was not allowing her to have ideas above her station and she tried to remember if at any time she had omitted to call him 'my Lord' while they had been talking.

She told herself that she must be very very careful.

'If I speak as if I am an equal, he will be suspicious of me,' she warned herself.

They returned to the stables.

When they had dismounted, Kyla told Jane in a low voice,

"Thank your uncle for such an enjoyable ride."

"Thank you, Uncle Rollo. That was lovely. Please may I ride with you again? It is much more exciting than going out with one of the grooms."

"I am glad about that," the Earl smiled.

"I want to thank you too," Terry said, having received a little push on the shoulder from Kyla. "It was the most exciting ride I have ever had. I think your horses are scrumptious."

The Earl grinned.

"I have watched you ride," he said, "and I believe that we can give you a bigger horse tomorrow."

"I would like that, my Lord," Terry exclaimed.

The two children found Kyla and, as she was beginning to walk away, the Earl said,

"By the way, Miss Taylor, will you please tell Nanny that I had almost forgotten that a Lady Shenley is calling on her this afternoon."

He spoke quite casually.

Then he was aware that Miss Taylor had suddenly stiffened and was standing very still.

She could not believe what she had just heard.

Then she asked in a voice that sounded strained,

"You did say – Lady Shenley – my Lord?"

"Yes, that is right," the Earl said. "She wants to see The Castle and especially Nanny, who, she told me, had been Nanny to her stepchildren."

He was looking at Kyla as he spoke and it seemed to him that the colour had gone from her face completely.

In a voice that he could hardly hear, she replied,

"I will – tell Nanny – what your Lordship has said."

She turned away hastily and moved towards The Castle. The Earl saw her take hold of the small boy's hand and then draw him, he thought, with unnecessary haste over the cobbled yard.

Then he told himself that he must be imagining it.

There was no way that he could think of in which Lady Shenley could be connected with Miss Taylor or, for that matter, with Lady Blessingham's grandson.

He stopped for a few minutes to speak to his Head Groom.

By the time he had walked towards the Castle, there was no sign of the children or Miss Taylor.

They had rushed up the stairs at a breathless speed to reach the nursery where Nanny was waiting for them.

"Have you had a nice time – " she began.

As soon as she saw Kyla's face, she asked rapidly,

"What has happened? What has upset you?"

Kyla went down on her knees beside the chair where Nanny was sitting.

"His Lordship – has told me to – tell you," she said in a trembling voice, "that – Lady Shenley is coming here this – afternoon to – see you."

"To see me?" Nanny asked.

Then, before Kyla could reply, she added,

"I told you this would happen. Now Terry and you will have to hide."

Jane had gone to her bedroom and Betty, the nursery maid, was waiting there to help her out of her riding clothes.

Terry ran over to Nanny, who had risen to her feet.

He clung to her.

"You won't let her find us, will you, Nanny?" he asked. "You know Stepmama is going to kill me."

Nanny put her finger to his lips.

"Be careful what you say," she urged. "You must not let Betty hear anything like that."

Terry glanced apprehensively towards Jane's room.

"What shall we do?" Kyla whispered.

"Behave normally," Nanny said quietly, "as long as Betty is about. As soon as Jane goes to rest after luncheon, I'll hide you both."

"What will his Lordship say to Stepmama if she asks him questions?" Kyla whispered. "It will seem strange if Miss Taylor and Lady Blessingham's grandson suddenly disappear."

"Leave it to me," Nanny proposed.

As she spoke, the door of Jane's room opened and she said in a louder voice,

"I suggest that you go to change, Miss Taylor. Luncheon'll be up very shortly and Gerald must take off his ridin' boots and wash his hands."

Kyla did as Nanny told her.

When she reached her bedroom, Terry came running after her.

He pushed the door shut behind him and flung himself into her arms.

"Let's – run away, Kyla, before Stepmama – arrives," he pleaded. "I don't want to – be killed. I want to live and ride – wonderful horses like I was riding this morning."

"Now we have to be brave," Kyla said. "I know exactly what Nanny is planning. We will go into the secret passages and stay in the Priest's Hole until Stepmama has gone away."

Terry had obviously not thought of this solution.

"Hide in the Priest's Hole," he said. "That is a clever idea. She will never find us there."

"The Earl will not think that is where we are likely to be," Kyla said, "because no one is supposed to know of the secret passages except for himself."

"We will be – all right there," Terry insisted confidently.

"Of course," Kyla said, "and you will have to be very very brave and look after me as well as yourself."

"I will do that," Terry replied, "but I want my pistol. Can we take our pistols with us?"

Kyla nodded.

Then she said,

"It will upset all Nanny's plans if Betty or anyone else is suspicious. Go and change your boots as Nanny said and be very careful what you say at luncheon."

Then she kissed her brother and carried on,

"I am sure Papa and Mama will look after us and will not let that horrible woman – hurt us. After all we were very lucky to get – here safely."

"Yes, we came here," Terry agreed, "but I am still – afraid, Kyla."

"So am I," she replied. "But we must not let anyone know."

"I will try – to be brave," Terry smiled weakly.

As he went from the room, Kyla felt the tears coming into her eyes.

He was too young, much too young, to be involved in anything as horrible as this.

She knew that he was trying very hard to be brave, although he was very afraid, just as she was, of what their stepmother might do to them.

Kyla changed her clothes and then went back into the nursery.

Luncheon had just been brought in by two footmen and Kyla was much relieved to see that Betty had disappeared.

The footmen served their luncheon and they talked about the Earl's horses.

It seemed to take a very long time because Kyla found it difficult to eat anything.

She could only pray that Nanny had everything planned out in her mind.

They could start to hide as soon as the footmen had taken the used plates and what was left of the luncheon downstairs.

As Nanny rose from the table, she said to Jane,

"Now you must be tired after havin' so long a ride. If you want to go to your house in the trees later on this afternoon, you must have a good rest. So hop into bed and try to sleep."

"Can we take our tea to my house in the wood?" Jane asked.

"I will think about it," Nanny answered. "Just you close your eyes and be a good girl, otherwise you will be too tired to enjoy it."

"I will try," Jane promised.

Nanny took her into her bedroom and undressed her.

Betty had by now gone downstairs for her luncheon.

When Nanny came back into the nursery, Kyla and Terry were waiting for her. They had not even spoken to each other since she had left them.

Nanny took charge at once.

"Now," she said. "You both have to disappear. You know exactly where to go."

"To the Priest's Hole," Kyla said.

"I have just been thinkin' what you'll want," Nanny went on, "which will be a couple of blankets and two pillows and I'll show you the little lantern that his Lordship has at all the entrances to the secret passages."

"What about food?" Terry asked.

"You can take with you the box of biscuits in the cupboard," Nanny said, "but, of course, I'll bring you some food if you're there long."

She looked at Kyla before she added,

"I hope her Ladyship'll only be droppin' in for tea," she commented.

"If you can convince her that you have not seen us or know anything about our having disappeared," Kyla answered, "I can see no reason why she should linger."

She thought for a few moments and then said,

"His Lordship said, 'tell Nanny a Lady Shenley is coming to see her.' I think that means he cannot know her as a friend but just as an acquaintance."

"I just hopes you're right," Nanny said. "Now, come along, both of you. I've two extra blankets in my room in case it gets cold."

She gave Kyla one of the blankets to carry and took the other one herself, while Terry managed the two pillows.

There was no one in the passage outside the nursery because the staff were all having their luncheon in the servants hall.

They slipped into the big cupboard and Nanny turned the lock and opened the trap door after she had taken away the woollen rug.

Then she bent down and took from the hook at the bottom of the steps a small lantern.

It had a wick, which was soaked in oil and attached to it was a tinderbox by which they could light the wick.

She showed them how it was done, saying as she did so that the Curator had explained it all to her.

"You'll not need it till it's dark," she told Kyla. "Be ever so careful not to drop it."

"I will be very careful," Kyla promised.

"I'll carry it now," Nanny said, starting to go down the ladder.

When she reached the bottom, Kyla dropped the other blanket down and the two pillows.

Then, when she and Terry had joined Nanny, they walked along the narrow passage until they reached the Priest's Hole.

"You'll be safe here," Nanny said. "If you take my advice, you'll have a lie down and try to rest. 'Tis no use agitatin' yourselves with what's happenin' outside."

"You will come to tell us as soon as she has gone?" Terry asked plaintively.

"Of course I will," Nanny answered. "And you must look after your sister and don't let her get upset. You have got to be as brave as your father would have been."

"It wasn't brave of Papa to marry her," Terry said. "She is a wicked, wicked woman and he should have been clever enough to know how bad she was."

It was what Kyla thought herself, but there was no point in saying so.

Nanny kissed Terry.

"You are a big boy," she said, "and we're all goin' to believe that everythin' is goin' to be all right."

"It will be as soon as Stepmama goes away," Terry said forcefully.

Nanny touched Kyla affectionately on the shoulder.

"Now, don't you upset yourself," she said in a low voice. "It'll all come right in the end. You mark my words."

"That is what I want to believe," Kyla sighed.

"I've left the biscuits in the cupboard," Nanny exclaimed. "Now, come along, Terry, and fetch them from me. Then I'll shut the trap door and no one'll have any idea where you are."

She walked away as she did so.

When she and Terry were gone in the dim light, Kyla spread one blanket on the mattress of the Priest's bed.

She hoped that she and Terry would not have to sleep on it for a long time.

'I am sure that Stepmama will leave when she has seen Nanny and realises that we are not here,' she told herself reassuringly.

At the same time she knew that she was seriously afraid that something would go wrong.

Terry came back with the biscuits.

"Can I eat one now?" he asked.

"Yes, of course," Kyla replied.

Terry opened the box.

Then he said,

"Shall we explore the passages and see if we can peep through into any of the rooms?"

"No, of course not," Kyla replied. "Even if we took our shoes off, someone might hear us. We must just sit here or rather lie on this bed and only whisper because voices can carry."

Terry lay down on the bed and Kyla took one of the pillows and sat on the floor with her back to the wall.

Neither of them spoke and, after a little while, Kyla realised that Terry had fallen asleep.

It had been a strenuous morning and Kyla had the idea that, because he was so excited about riding the Earl's horses, he had not gone to sleep for a long time last night.

Quite suddenly she thought that perhaps his suggestion was not such a bad one.

If they could peep into some of the other rooms in the house, she might then be aware of what was happening when her stepmother arrived.

She took off her shoes and on stockinged feet she crept along the passage.

It was the one they had come on when Nanny had opened the secret panel in the library.

She had not gone at all far when she realised that there was what appeared to be a small door in the inner wall of the passage.

She pulled at it very cautiously.

Then she realised that it was a spyhole and she could see quite comfortably through it with one eye.

It looked into one of the rooms that led off the wide corridor, which ended in the hall.

There was no one in the room and Kyla could see, however, several beautiful pictures on the walls.

Beneath them stood gilded furniture which she knew had been designed by Adam.

She closed the small door and then moved on to the next one.

This one looked into the drawing room and, by moving her head, she could see two fine crystal chandeliers and a picture that she thought must be by Van Dyck.

She was just about to close the spyhole into the drawing room, when she heard a door opening.

Then there was the butler's voice saying,

"I'll tell his Lordship that you are here, my Lady."

Kyla drew in her breath.

Then with her eye to the spyhole she saw her stepmother.

She was very expensively gowned in a rustling silk and a bonnet trimmed with emerald-green ostrich feathers and there were diamonds that Kyla recognised had once belonged to her mother glittering in her ears.

She had come.

She was here!

Now Kyla could only pray frantically that the Earl would not somehow give them away.

Although they were supposed to have left The Castle, they could be found and captured.

As their legal Guardian, Lady Shenley would claim them and they would have to go with her.

'Please God – please let us be – safe,' Kyla prayed.

Then she heard the door open and the Earl came into the drawing room.

"Good afternoon, Lady Shenley," he started.

"Oh, my Lord, I very much hope that I don't disturb you," Lady Shenley said in her most appealing voice. "I have been so looking forward to this moment and your Castle is even more splendid than I expected it to be."

"And, of course, I must show you some of it," the Earl replied. "I think you also wanted to see the Nanny who is looking after my niece."

"I am sure that Nanny would be hurt if I visited here without doing so," Lady Shenley answered.

"Would you like to see her now or later?" the Earl enquired. "But first, of course, I must offer you some refreshment after your journey. Will you have a glass of champagne?"

As he spoke, the butler came into the room.

He was followed by a footman carrying a tray on which there were glasses and a bottle of champagne in an ice cooler.

"How very kind," Lady Shenley cooed. "I do find that driving in this hot weather rather exhausting."

"Who are you staying with in this part of the world?" the Earl asked.

"Actually with nobody," she replied, "but I am making a pilgrimage to the Churchyard at Dunlake."

The Earl knew that it was only a few miles from The Castle.

As he looked surprised, Lady Shenley explained,

"One of my dearest and most beloved friends is buried there. Every year I try to go when it is her birthday and put flowers on her grave."

Listening to her Kyla was quite certain that this was all completely untrue.

She could not imagine her stepmother doing anything so sentimental.

"I think it is very loyal of you," the Earl said, "and, of course, it is quite a long journey from London."

"Too long," Lady Shenley nodded, "and I hate staying in a Posting inn, as I am sure you do too, my Lord,"

"I never do stay in them if I can help it," the Earl said. "Fortunately I have a great friend who lives exactly halfway between The Castle and London, who is always delighted to see me. So I have a comfortable bed whatever time at night I may arrive."

"Oh, how lucky you are," Lady Shenley exclaimed. "My bed last night could have been used by a Fakir as a bed of nails and I really felt that I was expiating all my sins on it."

The Earl laughed.

"I cannot believe there are very many."

"Quite enough if my bed was anything to judge by," Lady Shenley replied.

Although she could not see them, Kyla was sure that they were seated side by side on the sofa.

She realised that her stepmother was trying to make the Earl invite her to stay and she hoped that he would not be beguiled into asking her to be his guest.

'If he does,' she thought frantically, 'we shall just have to stay here in the dark until she leaves and perhaps it will be difficult for Nanny, whatever she may say, to bring us any food.'

Her stepmother made a few more remarks about the discomfort of travelling in the hot weather.

Then the Earl suggested,

"If you have finished your champagne, shall we go upstairs to the nursery? I could send for Nanny, but I expect that you would prefer to see her in her own environment."

"Yes, of course," Lady Shenley agreed. "How sensible of you to know that Nanny could never look in her right place except with a rocking horse, a doll's house and, of course, all her children around her."

"That is indeed true," the Earl said as he smiled, "and the rocking horse, I may tell you, is one I used myself when I was a child."

"Now I hear as well that your horses are the finest in England," Lady Shenley said. "That is something else I would like to see while I am here."

Listening, Kyla thought despairingly that, judging by the way she was behaving and, if the Earl was taken in by it, she would be staying at The Castle for weeks.

He had now risen to his feet and was moving under the chandelier towards the door.

"I am afraid that there are two flights of stairs," he said, "but that will be no difficulty for someone as young as yourself."

"Now you are flattering me," she said. "Which is something I may tell your Lordship, I much enjoy."

She was talking in a flirtatious voice that Kyla had heard so often.

Then, as they left the drawing room, she then closed the spyhole and tiptoed back to the Priest's Hole.

Terry was still fast asleep.

She knelt down in front of the Altar.

She closed her eyes and put her hands together.

She prayed with an intensity that she had never known before that she and Terry would be saved from a terrible Fate.

CHAPTER SIX

The Earl found it impossible to go to sleep.

He was going over and over what had happened since Lady Shenley had called to see him.

He had taken her upstairs himself to the nursery in the end.

He was surprised when he entered to see that Nanny was alone with his niece.

Lady Shenley moved forward and said in what he realised was a very affected tone,

"How delightful to see you, Nanny. I do hope you are well."

Nanny had risen to her feet and she responded in what was obviously a cold voice,

"Very well thank you, my Lady."

Lady Shenley looked round the nursery.

"What a charming room," she said. "And I see that you have your bedroom opening out of it."

Without asking permission, she walked to one of the bedroom doors.

She opened it and peeped inside.

The Earl thought that it was strange behaviour and, turning to Nanny, he enquired,

"Where are Gerald and Miss Taylor?"

"A carriage came for Master Gerald," Nanny replied, "from his grandmother, saying that she wished her sister, who is now somewhat better, to see him. As he was so reluctant to go, Miss Taylor accompanied him."

It was all that Nanny said.

But what she did say sounded, the Earl felt, as if she had thought it all out in advance.

He was about to say that it seemed a strange story.

Then he was aware of a pleading look in the elderly woman's eyes that he had not seen before.

The words that he was about to speak died on his lips.

As Lady Shenley came from the second room that she had opened, which was Jane's, she said,

"Do tell me, Nanny, have you seen dear little Terry and Miss Kyla lately?"

"I heard from them both at Easter, my Lady," Nanny answered.

Lady Shenley was looking at her piercingly.

"Are you quite certain that they have not been here?"

"I would certainly know if they had," Nanny replied in a somewhat hostile tone.

"Well, it has been nice to see you," Lady Shenley said, walking towards the door.

The Earl followed her and they went downstairs in silence.

Then he recalled that, as if she had suddenly made up her mind, she started to be very flirtatious.

In fact she made it quite obvious that she wanted to stay in The Castle.

He was, however, determined that she would not do so.

She stayed and stayed until it was impossible not to ask her to have dinner with him.

During the meal she deliberately, he thought, made it very clear to him that she found him attractive as a man.

As soon as they had left the dining room, he ordered her carriage.

She protested that it was going to be most uncomfortable in the Posting inn.

Nevertheless he firmly escorted her to the front door and there was nothing else that she could do but leave.

Now, as he thought over her behaviour, he found it more and more strange.

He was also certain that, while she might genuinely welcome him as a lover, which he had no intention of being, there was some other reason for her anxiety to stay in The Castle.

When he went upstairs to go to bed, Jenkins was waiting for him.

"Was Lady Shenley's coachman," the Earl asked, "given something to eat?"

"Yes, of course, my Lord," Jenkins replied. "He 'ad supper with us and,'e tells us that he's sick to death of this 'ere 'unt for 'er Ladyship's stepchildren."

"What do you mean, a hunt?" the Earl enquired.

"Apparently they've run away," Jenkins answered, "and, from all I 'ears, no one could blame them for doin' so. Her Ladyship be a real tartar."

The Earl was listening while he took off his evening clothes.

"How old are the stepchildren?" he asked when Jenkins finally paused for breath.

"I understands the young lady be nineteen and the boy be about eight," Jenkins replied.

The Earl did not say anything more.

But when he was in bed, he went over in his mind the conversation word by word.

He thought everything was beginning to fit together like in a jigsaw puzzle.

He remembered that Lady Shenley had mentioned the name 'Miss Kyla' and he thought that he had heard it before.

Then he remembered that it was when he visited the nursery on the day he arrived home.

Everything now fell into place.

At the same time the conclusion appeared too far-fetched and too melodramatic.

He thought that he must be telling himself a detective story.

Was it possible that Miss Taylor was really Lady Shenley's stepdaughter and the boy, who he had been told was the grandson of Lady Blessingham, her stepson?

'I am imagining it,' the Earl said to himself. 'Of course I am.'

He wished that he had asked Jenkins if Miss Taylor had returned to her home after taking young Gerald to visit his grandmother.

Then he had a sudden idea.

He rose from his bed and, lighting a candle, walked across the room to the fireplace.

He pressed a secret catch on one of the carved panels and it opened.

As he stepped through the aperture, he told himself that he was being ridiculous.

How was it possible for Miss Taylor and Gerald to be hiding in the secret passages?

No one in The Castle was supposed to know about them except for himself.

Yet he had always had the suspicion that some of the older servants, such as Mrs. Field, knew where they were.

Naturally, his Curator, who was away ill, and his secretary, Whitchurch, would be aware of their existence.

With bare feet the Earl moved down the passage.

He came to the flight of steps that led down to the Priest's Hole.

The passage went on farther along the front of the house.

He then went towards the Priest's Hole.

If anyone wanted to hide, it was the one place in the labyrinth of passages in The Castle where they could be more or less comfortable.

He had nearly reached the Priest's Hole, when he realised that there was a light coming from it.

He stopped, put down the candle he was carrying and went on without it.

When he reached the Priest's Hole, he moved very slowly and quietly.

He wanted to see what was happening inside.

If there was anyone hiding there, they would be frightened at his finding them.

The Priest's Hole was illuminated by one of the special oil lamps he had himself placed at the openings from the various rooms in The Castle.

By its light he could see the two people lying on the bed.

It was not hard to recognise the girl he had known as 'Miss Taylor' with her golden hair glinting in the light from the lantern.

She had her head on one of the pillows and was fast asleep.

Cuddled next to her with his arm across her, as if to protect her, was the boy purporting to be 'Gerald Blair'.

They were both dressed in their ordinary clothes and had a blanket over their legs and the boy had taken off his coat and was in his shirtsleeves.

The Earl stood looking at them without moving.

It suddenly struck him how young, innocent and vulnerable they both were.

As he looked at the girl, she did not seem much older than the boy he knew now was her brother.

She looked very helpless and quite suddenly the Earl felt that he wanted to protect her and to save her from what had made her appear so terrified.

He knew now that it was the dominating and determined woman who had just dined with him.

The Earl decided that the kindest thing he could do was to let Kyla and Terry believe that he had not discovered their secret.

He would very much hope that Lady Shenley would not return to The Castle.

Walking very slowly so that he did not waken the two refugees, he moved silently back the way he had come.

Picking up his candle, he reached his own room.

Before the Earl fell asleep, he told himself that the two young people would be quite safe with their old Nanny.

There was no likelihood, he thought, that Lady Shenley would find them here.

Unless, unfortunately, something had been said to make her suspicious.

*

Kyla awoke because she heard Nanny calling for her.

She opened her eyes and realised that the lantern was still burning brightly.

There was, however, also a faint light coming into the Priest's Hole from the outside.

"Get up," Nanny was saying. "Get up, Miss Kyla, and come back to your own room."

Kyla was suddenly awake.

"Do you mean it is safe?"

"Her Ladyship left after dinner," Nanny said, "and I intend to tell his Lordship that you and Terry came back while they were eatin' their meal."

Kyla jumped off the bed.

"You are quite certain it is safe?"

"It would seem very extremely strange if you had not returned," Nanny answered. "I told his Lordship that Terry had only gone to visit his grandmother and her sister so, of course, he would have come back with you."

"You don't think that Stepmama still suspects that we are here in The Castle?" Kyla said in a nervous voice.

"She couldn't find you and that should be enough," Nanny replied. "But we shall have to be on our guard in case she comes back unexpectedly."

Kyla thought this over while Nanny bent over the bed to wake up Terry.

"Come along," she was saying briskly, "you can get into your own bed now and be more comfortable than you were here."

"I was dreaming," Terry said sleepily. "What has happened?"

Then he opened his eyes and said in a frightened voice, "Has Stepmama gone?"

"She has really gone," Nanny said. "Let's all of us hope we have seen the back of her."

They climbed up the ladder into the cupboard.

"Now, go to bed, both of you," Nanny said. "I won't wake you until breakfast is on the table."

Terry yawned.

"I am very sleepy," he confirmed.

"I will come and undress you," Nanny answered.

She was just going into his room when Kyla gave a little cry.

"I have just thought of something, Nanny," she said.

"What is it?" Nanny asked. She was busy unbuttoning Terry's shirt.

"We must not go out while Stepmama is still in the vicinity," Kyla said. "She might see us and then we should be lost."

"That's true," Nanny replied as if she had just thought of it herself.

"I know what we can do," Kyla said. "We will get Bill, our highwayman, to find out for us where she is and if she has gone back to London. I know he would do it for us."

"How are you going to get hold of him?" Nanny asked.

Kyla told her how Bill had told them to put something red on the Magic Oak in the Park.

"And then he will meet me there when it is dark," she told her.

"That sounds a bit of common sense to me," Nanny remarked.

Kyla thought that it was more than that.

It was the one way for them to know that it was safe to go riding or even to play in the garden.

When she went to her room, she told herself that she must be very careful not to take any risks.

She was quite certain that, if her stepmother had them back into her clutches, there would be no escape.

The Earl actually was not surprised when only Jane joined him to go riding.

"Gerald is still asleep" Jane said. "Nanny says that yesterday was too much for him."

"What about Miss Taylor?" the Earl asked.

"She said that she had a bad headache and I was to ask you to excuse her from riding with us."

The Earl knew the real reason for the non-appearance of Miss Taylor and the boy who was called 'Gerald'.

He said nothing but merely took Jane with him.

They rode into the paddock and through the woods to the flat lands.

She enjoyed every moment of her ride.

When they had returned to The Castle, she thanked him very prettily for letting her ride with him.

"You are very kind, Uncle Rollo," she said, "and I love you nearly as much as I love Papa."

"If you are writing to your father this week," the Earl said, "tell him he must be very proud of how well you ride. You must also tell him that you are learning a lot with your new Governess."

"We have had only one lesson," Jane said, "and it was Arithmetic, so I did not like it."

"What do you like?" the Earl enquired.

"I like hearing the stories Miss Taylor tells me and Nanny tells me some too and they are exciting."

Jane went back into The Castle and the Earl was just leaving the stables when he saw someone coming towards him.

He gave an exclamation of delight.

It was Charles Sinclair, who had arrived, he thought, just when he needed him.

"I thought you would be pleased to see me," Charles announced. "I have come here at breakneck speed. I slept only for a very short time at a very uncomfortable Posting inn."

"Why did you not go to Carstairs, where I always stay?" the Earl enquired. "You know James would have been delighted to have you."

"I know that," Charles replied. "But it would have taken a great deal longer. I had the idea that you needed me urgently, although I don't know why."

The Earl smiled.

It was a kind of instinct that they had had about each other during the War and which still lingered on in Peace.

When they were back in London, he only had to think about Charles to bring him from his lodgings to Berkeley Square.

So there was really no need to send a groom with a note.

"Yes, I do want you, Charles," he said. "And I have something to tell you that I think you will find really interesting."

He took Charles into the study.

While he was having some coffee, which he had asked for when he arrived, the Earl told him about Lady Shenley.

Charles Sinclair listened attentively.

And then he said,

"I have heard quite a lot about that woman. She has quite a bad reputation amongst the Dowagers and is, I think, living with a very unpleasant man called 'Hunter'."

"I think I know him," the Earl said. "He is a bad lot. On one occasion he was accused of cheating at cards."

"I should imagine that he cheats at a great number of things," Charles replied. "Now that I think about it, I did hear that several people thought it strange that Lord Shenley died for some reason the doctors could not diagnose while he was still a comparatively young man."

The Earl thought for a moment and then he said,

"If Lady Shenley wanted to get rid of her husband to marry Hunter, why should she be so concerned about her stepchildren?"

'Hunter has no money. Not a penny," Charles replied. "And I imagine that what Shenley had is all left to his son."

The Earl frowned.

"It still does not seem to make sense to me," he said. "You would have thought that if they had run away, Lady Shenley would have been glad that they were off her hands."

"Why do you not face the girl with the truth and then ask for an explanation?" Charles enquired.

"Because she is already very frightened," the Earl answered, "and if she thinks that I am over-inquisitive or finding fault, she and the boy might run away from here. At least they are safe here with their dear old Nanny."

"I see your reasoning," Charles replied, "in which case we must just play it off the cuff."

"That is what I thought," the Earl agreed.

*

Kyla slipped down the drive when the servants were busy in the kitchen and the pantry and the Earl was having luncheon with his friend.

She told Nanny that she would be back before anybody would even notice that she had left The Castle.

She reached the Magic Oak and was relieved to see that there was no one about.

She wondered if there were many more emblems added to those which had been already hanging from the bough.

As she looked round the huge tree, she gave a gasp.

On one of the most conspicuous boughs there was a red handkerchief.

And she knew at once that it must have been put there by Bill.

There was therefore no need to use the red ribbon that she had brought, which Nanny had found for her in one of the nursery drawers.

He will be here as soon as it is dark, she told herself and hurried back to The Castle.

Because she was worried and anxious as to why Bill should want her, Kyla felt that the hours went by very slowly.

The Earl and his friend came up to the nursery after tea.

Although the Earl introduced her to Mr. Sinclair, he spent most of the time talking to Jane and Terry.

Kyla had no idea that the real reason for the visit was for Charles Sinclair to see her.

She would certainly have been embarrassed if she had heard Charles say as the two men went downstairs,

"Good Heavens, Rollo, the girl is a beauty! I suppose because she has been in mourning for her father she has not yet burst into the Social world. She will certainly create a sensation when she does!"

"I think she has a very unusual face," the Earl replied, "and that she rides better than any woman I have ever seen."

"Well, I should imagine that her stepmother is very jealous of her," Charles remarked, "if nothing else."

The Earl did not answer.

He found himself feeling sure that it was something more than that, yet he could not put a name to it.

Because they were always content to be together, the two men sat and talked in the study before dinner.

They went into the dining room and they were laughing.

When the meal was finished, they went back into the study and the Earl suggested,

"Would you like a game of piquet or backgammon?"

"I think I would rather talk to you," Charles said. "I missed our conversations when you were in Paris and I have still some amusing gossip to tell you about our friends."

The Earl laughed.

"Well, go ahead. Here is a glass of old brandy to loosen your tongue."

He handed a glass to Charles as he spoke and took one himself.

As he sat down in a comfortable chair, the door opened and to his surprise Miss Taylor came in without being announced.

She closed the door behind her.

Then, as the two men rose to their feet, she looked at the Earl and said,

"Please, my Lord, can I talk to you?"

"Of course," the Earl answered. "Anything you have to say can be said in front of my friend, Charles Sinclair, whom I would trust with my life, if necessary, as I have done since the War."

Kyla came a little nearer to them both.

Then she said, looking at the Earl,

"If I tell you the truth, the whole truth, will you promise to believe me?"

The Earl looked at her and replied very quietly,

"I promise I will believe everything you tell me."

*

Kyla had gone to the Magic Oak earlier than Nanny had thought sensible.

"It's only just nine o'clock," she said, "and I doubt if that highwayman'll be waitin' for you till it's really dark."

"I feel that he has something urgent to tell me" Kyla said. "I think he is somewhere in the woods on the other side of the drive"

Nanny did not argue, she merely lent Kyla a cape made in a dark material, which would make her less conspicuous.

Kyla slipped out of the house by a side door and she hurried down the drive, keeping near to the bushes.

The sun had already sunk and the first evening stars were coming out in the sky.

She hurried along hoping that no one would notice her.

If they did, she hoped that they would think she was just a girl returning to the village.

She reached the Magic Oak and stood gazing at the red handkerchief.

It was still tied round the bough.

It was then that she heard a whistle from the other side of the drive and knew who it was.

She hurried from the tree.

Pushing her way through several bushes, she then found Bill seated on Samson among the tall trees.

When he saw her, he dismounted and tied the reins as he had done when they had first met.

As he moved towards Kyla, she said,

"Oh, Bill, I am so pleased to see you. I came to the tree this afternoon to put a red ribbon on it, hoping that you would see it, and then I saw yours."

"I were afraid you'd forgotten our arrangement," Bill said.

"No, of course, I had not," Kyla answered.

Then she looked up at him and said,

"What has happened? What have you to tell me?"

"Bad news!" Bill replied.

There was a fallen tree lying beside them and he sat down on its trunk.

"Now come and listen to what I've to tell you," he ordered.

Kyla sat down next to him and, as she did so, she said,

"I have a feeling you know that my stepmother is in the vicinity."

"I knows about 'er," Bill said. "And that's what I 'as to tell you."

Kyla clasped her hands together.

"This is just what I wanted you to find out," she said.

"I finds out right enough," Bill answered, "but I'm afraid it'll frighten you."

"Tell me, tell me what – you have discovered," Kyla pleaded.

Bill told her that not far from The Castle there was an inn where the highwaymen like himself knew that it was safe to go.

"I were in there last night," he said, "'avin' a wee bite to eat, 'cos I've been fortunate in gettin' the money to pay for it."

"Oh, Bill, do be very careful!" Kyla said involuntarily. "I am so frightened that someone might capture or kill you."

"I'll be careful," Bill said, "not only of the gentry as I wishes to rob, but of me own kind, so to speak."

Kyla looked at him questioningly and he explained,

"There's 'ighwaymen and 'ighwaymen, and some of them be scum, as I'm ashamed to be connected with."

~148~

He then went on to tell Kyla how, when he was at the inn, three highwaymen, whom he disliked, came in.

"I 'ears them comin'," he said, "and knows by their voices who they be, so I tips me 'at over me nose and pretends to be asleep."

"And they were not suspicious that you were awake?" Kyla asked.

Bill shook his head.

"They goes to the other end of the room and talks low but I 'ears what they be saying."

"What were they saying?"

"They says as 'ow Black Jack, 'e were the worst of them 'ad been approached by a woman called Lady Shenley, who 'as a stepdaughter called 'Kyla' and also a stepson called 'Terry'."

Kyla gave a little gasp and Bill went on,

"I knows who they were talkin' about and I made sure I didn't miss a single word."

"What did they say?" Kyla asked in a frightened voice.

"This Lady who be your Stepmama then tells Black Jack to snatch you away from 'Is Lordship when you be out ridin' with 'im."

Kyla drew in her breath, but she did not want to interrupt and so Bill carried on,

"'Er says 'er'll pay 'im five 'undred pounds for the boy and a thousand if 'e be killed in a struggle."

Kyla gave a cry.

"Oh, no, Bill!" she exclaimed.

"That be what Black Jack says and 'e adds, 'I told the woman we're not takin' any risks of 'anging on the gibbet, but a thousand pound be a thousand pound'."

"What did the other men say?" Kyla asked in a whisper.

"Jack tell them and the Lady says 'er'll give three 'undred pounds for you and there be no reason for them to injure you in any way and they agreed that three 'undred pound be a lot of money."

He began to explain exactly how they had planned it.

Apparently Lady Shenley's coachman had learnt from one of the servants that the Earl had taken Jane, the boy and their Governess out riding early in the morning.

"They'll be waitin' in the woods outside the flat lands," Bill said. "They'll take the Earl by surprise knowing that 'e won't be armed. There'll be nothin' 'e can do when they takes you away with them."

Kyla did not answer and after a moment he said,

"I'm sorry, me dear, I tells you all this, but I thinks as you 'as to know that 'er's a wicked woman who'll not give up till 'er gets you."

"I know that," Kyla said. "If we do not go riding tomorrow or the next day, they will get hold of us sooner or later."

"That's what I thinks meself," Bill agreed. "And Black Jack'll never give up so long as there be enough money waitin' for 'im."

"Thank you for telling me," Kyla said. "You have been a real friend and I shall never forget that you have tried so 'ard to help us."

She put out her hand as she spoke and Bill then said,

"I wish I could 'elp you more than just givin' you bad news. You're a real lady and I'm proud to know you!"

Kyla rose to her feet.

For a moment Bill did not move.

"What are you goin' to do, miss?" he asked.

"I am going to tell the Earl what you told me," Kyla said. "I cannot believe that he will allow Terry to be murdered or me to be taken away by my wicked stepmother."

"'E'll not give you over to 'er thinkin' as 'er's your Guardian and 'e wishes to 'ave no part in it?" Bill asked slowly.

Kyla shook her head.

"No," she said. "He has been a soldier and a very brave one and I know he will fight evil the same way that he fought Napoleon."

Bill rose to his feet.

"Well, I've done all I can," he said, "but I'm worried aboot you. Real worried, as if you was me own."

"I will tell you what I want you to do, Bill," Kyla said. "Will you come with me to The Castle and wait so that the Earl can speak to you himself and know that I am not making up this story? It does sound too fantastic to be true."

"I understands what you're sayin'," Bill said, "but suppose 'is Lordship 'as I clapped in irons and taken orf by the Magistrates. Where would I be then? And where would Samson be without me?"

"He will not do that, I know he will not. I trust him and I know that you can trust him too."

She put her hand on his arm.

"Please, Bill, do this for me. I am so afraid that he will not believe me."

Bill thought for a moment and then he said grudgingly,

"Ah, well. But I 'opes you knows what you're a-doin', puttin' me 'ead in a noose."

'It is nothing like that, I swear it," Kyla tried to assure him

She walked with him, leading Samson through the woods until they were much nearer to The Castle.

Then, going through the same side door, she went in search of the Earl.

She finished telling her story while the Earl and Charles Sinclair sat in absolute silence.

Then she looked at them piteously and said,

"Perhaps I am wrong to ask your help in something as serious as this. We cannot stay hidden in The Castle for ever and. when we do come out, the highwaymen will be waiting."

The Earl jumped to his feet.

There was a strange expression on his face.

Charles had seen it during the War when he was up against what seemed an unbeatable enemy.

"You were so right, Kyla," he said, "to tell me. May I now call you by your real name? I only wish that you had trusted me before, when I would not have allowed your stepmother to come into The Castle or her servants to learn what she wanted to know from my servants, of course inadvertently."

"I can hardly believe any woman can be so wicked," Charles exclaimed. "But, of course, I agree with Kyla. She and Terry cannot sit inside The Castle for ever, knowing that if they come out, the highwaymen have been paid, what is to them a colossal sum, to capture them."

"And to – kill – Terry," Kyla murmured beneath her breath.

"That is something that will never happen while I am here," the Earl insisted. "And you were quite right to tell Bill that he can trust me. I am going to talk to him now and I suggest that you stay here with Charles, who will give you something to drink. What you have heard must have been a dreadful shock."

Kyla put out her hand and held on to his.

"You will be – kind to Bill – will you?" she pleaded.

She looked at him and then continued,

"He is not really a proper highwayman, but a gardener who came back from the War to find that his wife had run away, his cottage had been given to others and nobody wanted to employ him."

"I understand," the Earl said. I promise you that I will be very kind, just as he has been very kind to you."

His fingers tightened on hers for a moment before he walked resolutely towards the door.

Charles stood up at once.

"I must obey my orders, Kyla," he said, "and give you a glass of champagne. Let me tell you, I think you are

~153~

exceedingly brave. In fact the bravest woman I have ever met."

"I don't feel at all – brave," Kyla said in a low voice, "but I – felt that I could – trust the Earl. That he would – help me and would not hand us over to Stepmama because she is our Guardian – according to the Law."

"I can promise you that Rollo would never do a thing like that," Charles said. "He is my greatest friend and I have trusted him ever since we were schoolboys together."

He paused and then continued,

"I cannot tell you how magnificent he was when we were fighting the French or how many lives he saved, one way or another, by being intelligent including, of course, mine."

"Now he must – save Terry," Kyla muttered.

"And, of course, you," Charles answered.

"I do not – really – matter," Kyla replied. "If Stepmama – drugged me as she – intended to do, I only hope I should have had – brains left to – kill myself."

"You are not to talk like that," Charles insisted. "Now Rollo is in command, I promise you everything will be all right and your stepmother will be unable to hurt you in the future."

Kyla did not argue.

She could not help feeling, however, that even if the Earl saved her from this horrible plot, her stepmother would think up another.

She and Charles, who she thought was a very charming young man, sat talking.

Occasionally they lapsed into an anxious silence until the Earl returned.

When he came into the study, they both jumped to their feet.

Kyla spoke first.

"What has – happened? Has Bill – told you any – more than he – told me? Have you been – kind to him?"

"I will answer all your questions," the Earl said, taking her hand in his. "Now, come and sit down and don't be frightened, although I admit that you have every reason to be."

He pulled her towards the sofa and they sat down side by side.

The Earl did not relinquish her hand and Kyla thought that the strength and warmth of his grasp was very comforting.

"Bill has told me everything that you told me," he said in a quiet voice, "and added some information about Black Jack, which I found horrifying."

"You – mean," Kyla said in a very small voice, "that he has – killed people before?"

"One or two," the Earl admitted. "But I promise you he is not going to kill Terry or you or, for that matter, me!"

Kyla gave a little cry.

"I never thought of that. Oh, please be careful, my Lord. If anything happened to you, I would never – forgive myself for – embroiling you in this – wicked plot."

"Quite frankly," the Earl said, "if it was not that it frightened you, I should find it very interesting."

He looked at Charles as he went on,

"You know, Charles, we have often said how dull things are since the War has ended. Well, this is something when we have to use our brains to the full to protect ourselves from a very unpleasant enemy."

Charles, as if to relieve the tension, brought his hand up to his forehead in a salute.

"I am awaiting my orders. General," he burst out.

"It is serious, Charles," the Earl said somewhat reproachfully. "Equally I really do need you. We are now going to have a 'Council of War'."

He looked at Kyla and then said,

"But you, Kyla, are to go to bed. I want you to promise me that you will try to sleep and not worry about anything until we go off riding at nine o'clock after we have had a very good breakfast."

"How can you – expect me – not to worry?" Kyla asked him.

"I thought you trusted me," the Earl retorted.

"I do! You know I do," Kyla answered. "It is too much to – ask you, but I am so very – afraid for – Terry."

"Then we have a task," the Earl said, "which is to save you both, that is exactly what Charles and I intend to do. And, without boasting, what we *will* do."

"You are so – kind," Kyla murmured, "and I have – been so – very very frightened."

She looked up at him with tears in her eyes.

The Earl had an urgent impulse to put his arms round her and hold her close.

He wanted to tell her that he would protect her and make very sure that she never had to worry so much again.

But to do so he knew that it might upset her more than she was already.

Instead he drew her to her feet and he then raised her hand which he was still holding to his lips.

"Go to bed, Kyla," he ordered, "and when you say your prayers, which I am very sure you always do, ask your Guardian Angel to look after us all."

"I pray every – night and I feel now – because you are here – my prayers have all been – answered."

'That is what I wanted you to say," the Earl replied. "Now go upstairs and I think that it would be very sensible if you did not talk to Nanny or anyone else about what has happened tonight. Let it be a secret between us three."

"I will do – that," Kyla said. "Thank you, thank you – with all my heart."

Her voice broke on the words as he opened the door for her to leave the room.

She turned her head away so that he would not see her tears.

He thought, as he watched her hurry down the corridor, that she was far braver than any woman he had ever known.

Then he went back into the study and to Charles's surprise rang the bell.

CHAPTER SEVEN

Kyla found it impossible to sleep.

Having drawn back the curtains, she lay watching the stars gradually fading from sight.

She was feeling extremely apprehensive of what tomorrow would bring.

At the same time she felt confident that the Earl would manage to cope with whatever horrors her stepmother had planned for them.

'He is so strong and – so kind,' she told herself.

She remembered how, when he had kissed her hand, she had felt a strange feeling within her breasts.

It was something that she had never known before in her life.

Even to think of it brought the feeling back to her again and again.

She wondered why he seemed so different from any other men she had ever met.

It then struck her, and it was a surprise, that perhaps she was falling in love.

It was such a strange idea that she almost at once repudiated it, thinking it ridiculous.

Then she thought of the Earl and how handsome he was.

And how at the same time he had an authority about him that made everybody obey him.

She knew that he meant something to her that she could not put into any form of words.

When she had learnt what her stepmother had planned, she had gone to him instinctively.

It was not just because there was no one else, rather because she believed that, if anyone could save Terry and herself, it would be he.

'And that is what he will do,' she mused.

Again she felt that strange sensation flooding over her like a tidal wave.

She knew that, if she could do as she wished, she would run to the Earl.

Even to be near him would make her feel safe and not so terrified.

'Is it – love that I – am feeling?' she asked the stars above.

Then, because she had never known love and no man had ever meant anything to her, she was uncertain.

And yet the feeling persisted.

As the hours passed, she just closed her eyes and lay on the bed thinking all the time of the Earl.

She told herself how incredibly lucky it was that she and Terry had found him.

She must have dozed for a little while, for she awoke with a start as the door opened.

She saw that it was Nanny who was coming into the room.

The sun was now shining brightly, but it seemed strange to her that Nanny should come to her when she had not yet been called.

She sat up, asking,

"What has – happened, Nanny? Why are you – here?"

"It's all right, dearie," Nanny replied. "I've somethin' to tell you, so I came before Betty comes up to the nursery or anyone calls you."

Nanny smoothed the counterpane with her hand and then sat down on the bed.

"Now, listen to me, Miss Kyla," Nanny began. "Mr. Sinclair came up last night and gave me what you might call your orders for this mornin'."

"What did he say?" Kyla asked.

"His Lordship says you are to behave as if nothin' unusual was happenin'."

"What is happening?" Kyla demanded.

"You're goin' ridin' with his Lordship after breakfast."

Kyla gave a little cry.

"To meet the highwaymen?"

Nanny nodded.

"Mr. Sinclair says as you're not to be afraid, but what is important is that no one in The Castle should have any idea that everything's not happenin' as normally as it always does. His Lordship's afraid as her Ladyship might have someone spyin' for her."

Kyla drew in her breath.

"I never thought of that," she said. "But it is just the sort of thing that Stepmama would do."

"I know that," Nanny responded, "and that's why you're to do exactly what his Lordship wants and be ever so careful what you says in case anyone's listenin'."

"I will be careful – I will," Kyla assured her, "and we must tell Terry."

"He's still asleep," Nanny replied. "But I've told Mr. Sinclair how well you both shoot, so you are to take your pistols with you, though no one's to be aware of it."

Kyla put out her hand and took hold of Nanny's.

"I am so frightened, Nanny," she sighed.

"Of course you are," Nanny agreed. "But you'll be very brave, just as your mother would have been. And if you do as his Lordship says, I'm sure everything'll come right in the end."

"I do hope so," Kyla said beneath her breath.

Nanny left her and she started to dress.

As she did so, Betty came to call her, bringing her a cup of tea and a thin slice of bread and butter.

"Oh, you're up, miss," she exclaimed. "Well, I can't say as I blame you. It's a lovely day and it'll be real hot later on."

"That is what I thought," Kyla replied.

She took a few sips from the cup of tea.

She felt that, if she tried to eat anything, it would stick in her throat.

Then she remembered that, if she refused to eat any breakfast, it might cause comment.

'I must be so careful – very very careful,' she told herself as she finished putting on her riding habit.

Nanny had said that they were to take their pistols with them.

She thought that it would be a mistake, however, to take them to the nursery where they were to have breakfast.

She therefore left them where they were hidden in a drawer and she would pick them up before she and Terry went down to ride with the Earl.

When she reached the nursery, there was no sign of Jane.

She did not ask the question aloud, but Nanny must have read her thoughts, because she said,

"Jane's still sleepin' and I'm afraid she'll be disappointed she can't ride with you. But I'll tell her there'll be a surprise waitin' for her durin' the afternoon."

"What will that be?" Kyla asked.

"I'll think of somethin'," Nanny answered.

Terry ate a very hearty breakfast, whilst Kyla merely played with the eggs and bacon on her plate.

When it was a quarter to nine, she knew that it was time to go downstairs.

She kissed Nanny goodbye.

She did not say anything in case Betty was in the other room and might hear her.

Then she took Terry to her own bedroom.

"We are to take our pistols with us," she told him in a whisper, "but no one is to know that we are carrying them."

Terry tucked his in his trouser pocket, where it was hidden by his jacket.

While Kyla concealed hers under her riding coat.

Then they went downstairs and out through the front door and heading for the stables.

There was nobody about except for the two footmen on duty.

They walked in silence round the side of The Castle and under the archway that led into the stable yard.

They saw as they did so that the Earl was already there and the horses were just being brought from the stalls.

"Good morning, Miss Taylor," the Earl said politely. "Good morning, Gerald."

He, of course, addressed them in this way in front of the grooms.

"Good morning, my Lord," they both replied and Kyla dropped him a small curtsey.

"I thought it would interest you today," the Earl said, "to ride two of the horses I brought back from France. They are getting old now and they are not as fast as they used to be. But I am very fond of both of them and I think you will find them easy to handle."

Kyla looked at the horses he indicated.

She knew that, if they had been trained for warfare, they would be well used to gunfire and they would not bolt at the first explosion of a gun.

She thought that it was very clever of the Earl to remember that.

As she met his eyes, she felt that he could read her mind and was aware of what she was thinking.

He was looking at her so penetratingly that she felt herself blush.

She had no idea how attractive she looked as she did so.

"I think it's a spiffing idea to ride your charger," Terry was saying, "because it's much bigger than the one you gave me yesterday and I will feel like a General on him."

"Leading his troops," the Earl joked.

One of the grooms helped Terry into the saddle.

Kyla watched with a little stab of her heart as Terry looked very small and vulnerable on such a large animal.

She did not, of course, make any comment, she merely allowed a groom to help her onto the other horse.

If the horse had been, as the Earl had indicated, one of his chargers, it would be very obedient and do everything that was required of him.

He would also be quite unperturbed by anything unusual that might happen.

The Earl was riding the black stallion that he had ridden yesterday and she wondered if he would be able to hold it if there was any firing.

As she looked at the Earl, she thought that he was, without any exception at all, the most handsome man she had ever seen.

Astride the black stallion he might have been a God come down from Mount Olympus to lead them into battle.

The Earl was talking quite naturally to the grooms.

He ordered a slight adjustment to Terry's stirrups, which he thought looked a little too long.

He appeared to be in no hurry and was completely at his ease.

Kyla could feel the hardness of the pistol where it was concealed against her waist.

She was thinking that if it had not been there, she would have then been deceived into believing that they were simply going for a casual ride in the paddock.

Finally the Earl was satisfied that everything was ready and correct.

He rode forward and joined Terry, who had gone a little way ahead of him.

Kyla followed and they rode from the stable into the paddock.

She thought by this time that it must be after nine o'clock.

The highwaymen, led by Black Jack, would be waiting for them beside the flat land.

She felt her heart begin to beat frantically and she wondered how the Earl could look so calm.

Even Terry did not seem perturbed or agitated in any way.

The Earl waited until they reached the paddock before he drew in his horse and said,

"I want you both to listen to me."

They came as near to him as they could and he went on,

"You will both have to be very brave. When the highwaymen do approach us, they will be confident that we have not the slightest idea that we are expecting them."

"I hope – you are – right," Kyla murmured.

"What I want you to do," the Earl continued, "is to ride one on either side of me, Terry on my left and Kyla on my right."

He paused and then continued,

"Hold your reins low in your left hand and in your right hand you will hold your pistol, keeping it out of sight until I tell you to shoot."

Kyla gave a little cry.

"We are – to shoot?" she questioned.

"When I tell you to," the Earl answered. "And this is very important – you are to aim at the right arm of the Highwayman facing you."

He looked at Terry as he continued,

"Your Nanny tells me that you are both good shots and it is extremely important that the highwaymen should not be killed but only maimed. Do you understand?"

"I understand, my Lord," Terry agreed, "and so I will aim for his right arm and nowhere else."

"Good!" the Earl approved. "And you, Kyla, will do just the same. Your man's arm, of course, will be on the inside as he rides towards you. You must be careful to leave the one in the centre, who I think will be Black Jack, to me."

"I – understand," Kyla stammered.

"Very well," the Earl said. "Now, if you are both ready, we will ride on just as if we are enjoying the early morning sunshine."

"You don't think," Terry suggested, "that they will kill me before you can stop them?"

"I promise you there is no chance of that," the Earl said, "so long as you do exactly as I tell you. Shoot the moment I give the order and not a moment before."

When he had finished speaking, he looked at Terry and added quietly,

"I am very proud of you and of the way you are behaving as I know your father would be."

Kyla saw Terry straighten his shoulders and smile.

She felt the tears come into her eyes because the Earl was being so kind and thoughtful.

He did not speak to her again until they reached the trees at the far end of the paddock.

Then, as they began to move through them onto the flat ground, the Earl gazed at Kyla and said,

"You look very lovely. Are you still afraid?"

"I would be – if I was not – with you," Kyla replied without thinking.

Then, as she saw the expression in the Earl's eyes, she blushed and looked ahead.

There was no one in sight.

The sunshine made the flat ground, with trees on either side of it, seem very attractive.

It was quite impossible to believe that anything terrible could happen there.

"Chins up!" the Earl called out. "Here we go and God be with us!"

He moved forward as he spoke and Kyla and Terry kept pace with him on their large horses.

A minute later the highwaymen suddenly appeared as if from nowhere.

They rode out onto the flat land from behind the trees on the right hand side.

They then trotted slowly, keeping even with each other, towards the Earl.

They appeared not to be carrying pistols with them.

Kyla, however, suspected that they were holding them low on top of their saddles as they were doing themselves.

As she glanced at the Earl, she could see the barrel of his pistol just showing at the side of his riding coat.

The highwaymen were coming nearer and still nearer.

Just as Kyla thought that they were about to raise their pistols, the Earl ordered sharply,

"Shoot!"

As he gave the order, he raised his own pistol and shot Black Jack in the arm, just below the shoulder.

Black Jack gave a scream of pain and his pistol dropped from his hand.

Kyla's bullet caught the highwayman coming towards her a few inches above the elbow.

He acted in just the same way as Black Jack. He tried to raise his arm and in doing so his pistol fell to the ground.

Terry had aimed at the highwayman in front of him and the small bullet had pierced his arm.

It might not have been completely effective, however, if at the moment that the Earl had called 'shoot' another gunshot had not rung out.

It came from the trees on the left of the field.

Then Charles Sinclair and Bill were riding swiftly towards them.

Charles's shot had been a long distance one.

But he had managed to hit the highwayman's arm well below the shoulder.

In the same way as the others, the highwayman tried to raise his arm up and in doing so dropped his pistol as well.

It was Black Jack who realised quicker than his two confederates the position they were in.

He turned his horse towards the trees on the right.

Guiding it with just one hand, while his injured arm hung useless, he rode straight for the trees.

There was a low hedge just in front of them and he spurred his horse to leap over it.

He was unaware that there was someone crouching behind the hedge, peeping through the ivy that covered the top of it.

Having set up the diabolical trap for her stepchildren, Lady Shenley had been unable to resist leaving her carriage to watch her dastardly plan come to fruition.

She had crept through the undergrowth and crouched down behind the hedge, where she could see but would not be seen.

Black Jack swept over the hedge.

His horse had a glimpse of something where he was about to land and tried to avoid it and in doing so he stumbled and, kicking out to stop himself from falling over, struck Lady Shenley and knocked her onto her back.

With his injured arm and the swerving motion of his horse, Black Jack was thrown.

He fell heavily, swearing as he did so, on top of Lady Shenley, who was already severely injured, and crushed her beneath him.

When Black Jack rode away, the highwayman who had been shot by Kyla followed him.

His arm was agonisingly painful and he was unable to direct his horse at all skilfully.

It jumped the hedge as Black Jack's horse had done and landed on top of the two people on the ground.

The highwayman then fell off.

As he did so, Jenkins and the Earl's Head Groom came up the field to the place where Lady Shenley had left her carriage.

They dismounted and ran towards the two fallen men with ropes in their hands.

Before they could realise what was happening or recover from their fall, the highwaymen found themselves bound hand and foot and incapable of moving.

Terry had not moved as the two highwaymen had ridden off.

He was keeping watch over the third, who was groaning in pain with the two bullets in his arm.

He made no attempt to follow them, but said,

"All right, 'tis a fair cop and I wants a doctor right now for me arm."

"You will be lucky if you don't find a noose around your neck!" the Earl remarked.

Charles had drawn up his horse beside him and he said to him,

"Tie this man up. The grooms will be here soon to take him and the other two devils in front of the Magistrates. Incidentally, Charles, that was a *damned* good shot!"

"That is what I thought myself," Charles replied rather smugly.

Bill, who was standing a little way back, did not speak.

He bent forward to pat Samson's neck as if to show that he was thankful that neither his horse nor he was injured.

The Earl looked at him and rode to his side.

"I just cannot tell you how grateful I am," he said, "but I am short of a gardener at the moment and I also have an empty cottage."

Bill looked at him as if he could hardly believe what he was hearing.

"D'you mean that, my Lord?" he asked in a hoarse voice.

"I think you will find there is room for your horse in my stables," the Earl said, "and he will certainly be at home among his equals."

Bill laughed as if he could not help it.

"I knowed your Lordship would appreciate Samson."

"I do indeed and I also appreciate his owner. As it would be a huge mistake for anyone to know that you have been mixed up with this unpleasant gang, I suggest you ride back to The Castle and ask my Head Gardener to show you the cottage."

"I don't know what to say," Bill said in a broken tone.

"You can say it all later," the Earl said. "Go now. Some of my people will be arriving to collect this scum and take them to prison."

He glanced towards the hedge where he could see Jenkins and his Head Groom and he was sure that they were tying up Black Jack and the other highwaymen.

He saw too that the horses that had fallen were now riderless amongst the trees.

Charles had now finished tying up the third highwayman, who was lying on the ground, alternately groaning and swearing.

When Charles straightened himself, the Earl suggested,

"Look after Kyla and Terry for a moment while I go and see what is happening."

Without really thinking, Kyla dismounted and said to Charles in a low voice,

"The man's arm is bleeding very badly. Do you think I ought to do something about it?"

"Certainly not," Charles replied. "If you had been his victim, I can assure you he would have done nothing about you. Rollo has everything arranged and a wagon will soon be taking them to the nearest prison."

"The Earl was – wonderful," Kyla said beneath her breath.

It had all happened so quickly.

She could hardly believe now that they had defeated the highwaymen without their firing a single shot.

There had been no risk of either Terry or her being taken prisoner.

The Earl came riding back from the hedge.

She had heard him speaking to Jenkins and his Head Groom, but could not hear what he was saying.

When he joined them, he dismounted and gave Charles the reins of his stallion.

Then he moved close to Kyla and said in a low voice,

"It is all over. There is no need for you to worry anymore. Your stepmother is dead."

Kyla stared at him wide-eyed.

"When Black Jack jumped the hedge, she was hiding behind it. His horse knocked her over and kicked her and then Black Jack fell very heavily on top of her. Jenkins, who is very experienced in these matters, tells me that she is no longer breathing."

"I-I cannot – believe it!" Kyla murmured.

For a moment she stared at the Earl wildly.

Then she closed her eyes and felt as if the ground was rising up towards her.

The Earl put his arms round her and held her for a moment.

Then he turned to Charles,

"I will take her back to The Castle. You look after everything for me now."

Charles smiled.

"Very good, General! Anyway I congratulate you on a very successful battle."

The Earl did not answer.

He merely pushed Kyla gently into Charles's arms and mounted his stallion.

When he had done so, Charles gently picked Kyla up and placed her on the front of the Earl's saddle.

The Earl held her close against him with his left arm.

Turning his horse, he began to ride slowly and carefully back the way they had come.

Kyla had not completely fainted and now she felt the impending darkness moving away.

As Charles picked her up, her riding hat fell from her head and only when the Earl had moved away did he notice it lying on the ground.

She put her head on the Earl's shoulder.

She was vividly aware of the closeness of his body and it was indefinably comforting.

As if the Earl knew what she was feeling, he said,

"It is all right. It is all over. You are now safe, my darling, and no one shall ever hurt you again."

For a moment Kyla was still and then she looked up at him.

"What did you – call me?" she whispered.

"I called you 'my darling'," the Earl said, "which you have been ever since that first moment I saw you and wondered why you were so frightened."

They had by now reached the trees at the end of the flat land and then the Earl drew his stallion to a standstill.

"I love you!" he insisted. "I have loved you more and more every moment since I found you disguising yourself as a Governess."

"Y-you – *love me*!"

There was a note of elation in her voice that was like the song of the birds.

"I love you as I have never loved anyone before," the Earl admitted.

He bent his head and his lips found hers.

It was a very gentle kiss because he was afraid of frightening her.

But to Kyla it was as if he carried her into the warmth of the burning sun.

"I love – you! *I love – you!*" she wanted to say to him.

But it was impossible because the Earl was kissing her at first very gently and then more possessively.

"You are mine," he said as he raised his head. "Mine and I will never lose you. I was more frightened than I have ever been in my whole life that something would go wrong."

"You – were absolutely wonderful," Kyla murmured. "No one else could have – been so brilliant or planned – everything so cleverly."

"I did not plan your stepmother's death," the Earl said, "but I do think we can both thank God that she will no longer be able to threaten you."

"I did really think that, even if the highwaymen were unsuccessful, she would somehow contrive to get me back into her clutches."

"Because I had already thought of that," the Earl said, "I intended to marry you tonight in my Private Chapel so that it would be impossible for her to ever take you away from me."

"But – she might have got hold of – Terry and now that she is – dead and we can be happy."

"Very happy," the Earl agreed. "But I am still going to marry you, if not tonight, perhaps tomorrow or the next day."

Kyla gave a little cry.

"Are you sure – completely sure – you wish to – marry me? You don't – know me."

"I know all I want to know and I know what you make me feel," the Earl replied. "And I think, unless I am mistaken, that you love me a little."

"I – did not – realise it was – love until just now" Kyla said, "but I do love you – I love you with all my heart and soul – it is the most delightful exquisite feeling that I have – ever known."

The Earl laughed.

"That is exactly what I wanted you to tell me and now, as this is rather uncomfortable for you, I am taking you home."

Kyla made a little murmur.

Because he understood, he said,

"I know that ever since your father and mother died you have had no real home but The Castle is now yours as it is mine and we will make it a perfect place, not only for Terry but for our children as well."

Kyla put up her hand to touch his cheek.

"How can – you say – such wonderful – marvellous things to me," she asked. "Suppose I am only dreaming – and I shall wake up?"

The Earl laughed again.

"You are not dreaming, my lovely one. You are very much awake and starting a new life with me."

"That is exactly – what I want," Kyla whispered.

*

When Charles and Terry came back to The Castle, it was nearly luncheontime.

They found the Earl and Kyla in the drawing room.

She had changed out of her riding habit into one of her simple muslin gowns.

She looked just so happy and so radiant that, when Charles started telling them what had occurred after they had left, he suddenly stopped.

"I have a feeling, Rollo," he said, "although I might be wrong, that something far more sensational has happened here."

Kyla looked shy as the Earl went on,

"You are quite right, Charles, and I do hope you are going to give us a decent Wedding present."

"That is the best news I have ever heard," Charles said as he smiled. "I knew as soon as I saw Kyla that she was just the right woman for you and I have never known anyone so brave. Congratulations and where is the champagne?"

"I knew you would ask," the Earl replied. "The servants brought it in, but we forgot to drink it."

"Well, I certainly need a drink," Charles said, "and I think Terry deserves one too."

"Are you saying," Terry asked Kyla, "that you are going to marry the Earl?"

"He has asked me to do so," Kyla answered, "and says that The Castle will be a lovely home for you."

"You mean I can live here?" Terry enquired. "That's really spiffing! I shall really enjoy it."

"And, of course, riding my horses," the Earl commented.

"I will love that and I will explore all the hidden passages," Terry said.

"Now, what made you think The Castle has secret passages?" the Earl enquired.

Terry looked at Kyla.

"It is all right," she said. "I am sure he knows that we hid in one when Stepmama came."

"I saw you as it happens," the Earl pointed out.

"You – saw us?" Kyla exclaimed.

"I did not believe for one moment the story that 'Miss Taylor' had taken 'Gerald' to see Lady Blessingham's sister," the Earl replied, "so I got up after I had gone to bed and walked down the secret passageway leading from my room and saw two little runaways fast asleep in the Priest's Hole."

"And we had no idea of it," Terry added.

He looked at his sister reproachfully.

"We never took our pistols," he said, "and if the highwaymen had found us, they might have killed us both."

"The highwaymen do not know about the secret passages," the Earl said firmly, "and you will please, neither of you, show them to anyone else."

"But you will not mind if I go in them, will you?" Terry pleaded. "It is a spiffing place to hide."

"I can see that I shall have to design a special badge for us to wear as 'Guardians of the Secret Passages'," the Earl laughed, "and I shall put you, Terry, in charge."

Terry gave a whoop of excitement.

"I shall like that!"

"Now, come along, young man," Charles said. "You and I have now to drink the health of the bride and bridegroom and wish that they will live happily and safely ever after."

"That is a jolly good toast," Terry approved, "and, of course, it is what we wish them."

He accepted a glass from Charles and, as he raised it, he said,

"It was Kyla who thought of coming here and Kyla who made friends with Bill so that he helped us."

"Your sister is a most remarkable woman," the Earl said, "and that is why I intend to marry her as quickly as possible so that she can never run away from me."

"That is – something I have – no wish to do," Kyla said in a low whisper.

"I know that, my darling," the Earl answered, "but I will not feel sure of you until you are actually my wife."

Charles raised his glass.

"To you both!" he toasted. "And, if that is the way you feel, what are we waiting for?"

"You are right," the Earl said, "and now that I think of it Lady Shenley's death will have to be announced, which means that Kyla and Terry will be in mourning."

Kyla looked at him in surprise.

Then the Earl said,

"No one is going to know and I mean no one, exactly what happened today. I know I can trust my Head Groom and Jenkins. No one else need ever be aware that you were threatened by highwaymen. It will appear only that in riding away from us they killed Lady Shenley."

"What about the Magistrates?" Kyla asked.

"I have told my Head Groom and Jenkins to say that it was they who fought with the highwaymen, who they thought were trying to steal some of my horses. The highwaymen themselves would gain nothing by denying this nor do I think that they will be in a condition to do so."

"That is extremely clever of you," Charles said. "It will be of much less interest to the newspapers than if it was thought that they were trying to attack you or were hand in glove with Lady Shenley."

"I am glad you approve, Charles," the Earl said. "The idea came to me out of the blue. I told Jenkins what I wanted and I know that he will carry out everything that I have suggested to the letter."

"As he did when we were in France," Charles said. "Telling this story will ensure there will be no scandal and therefore you and Kyla must be married before Lady Shenley's death is announced."

"I will send for my Chaplain immediately after luncheon," the Earl informed them.

"I hope you will also find a Wedding veil for Kyla," Charles suggested.

Kyla gave a little cry.

"I had not thought of that and perhaps you will be – ashamed of me because I don't look – smart enough to be your bride."

"You are so lovely that the angels themselves will be jealous whatever you are wearing," the Earl said in a low voice.

She looked up at him as he spoke and for a moment they forgot that there was anybody else in the room.

With an effort he said,

"If you suggest that you will not be properly dressed, that will be an insult to Mrs. Field and not me."

"Of course, Mrs. Field will have everything!" Kyla laughed.

"Except for the Granston jewels," Charles said, "and so naturally Rollo will arrange that you wear the lot!"

"Certainly not," Kyla protested. "I should look like a Christmas tree and I do so want to look lovely – for Rollo."

"No one could be lovelier," the Earl said firmly. "I hope, Charles, you have brought your decorations with you as I naturally shall be wearing mine."

"You might well have warned me that this sort of thing was going to occur," Charles complained, "but some of your decorations will be on my coat just as they are on yours."

"A Wedding! We are going to have a Wedding!" Terry exclaimed. "I know that Jane will enjoy every minute."

The Earl looked guilty.

"I had forgotten about Jane," he admitted. "Terry, run up the stairs and fetch her down for luncheon and then tell Nanny that we are having luncheon in the dining room and she is to come too."

"Nanny is going to have luncheon with us?" Terry asked.

"Of course," the Earl replied. "She has been a great help in all our plans and we must not neglect her."

"She will be very excited," Terry commented.

He ran from the room as Kyla said,

"Oh, thank you – thank you for being so kind to Bill. I am so glad that he does not have to be a highwayman anymore."

"Because I am so happy at finding you," the Earl answered, "I want everybody else in the world to be happy too."

"I am sure that Nanny, when she knows that we are to be married, will be planning to fit everything into the nursery besides Terry."

"Of course you realise," Charles interrupted, "the most important thing is that you will now need a new Governess."

Kyla laughed as the Earl proposed,

"I think we had better find a Tutor for Terry. He is old enough for one and if one small boy does not give him enough to do, he can teach Jane as well."

"I am sure Jane would love that," Kyla said, "and it would be better for Terry to have a man to look after him."

"The trouble with you, Rollo," Charles said, "is that you are a born planner and happy only when you are thinking of new ways to do things. I am nervous to think what next you will introduce into the quiet English countryside, besides, of course, a large number of little Rollos!"

Kyla blushed and the Earl said,

"You are not to make Kyla feel shy, but you are quite right, Charles, I am going to plan a great number of different things, including building on to The Castle as my ancestors have always done."

"And there are causes I would want you to fight for in the House of Lords," Kyla said, "particularly to help the men like Bill, who have come back from the War to find their jobs have gone and, since they have no money, have to take to robbery."

"Quite right," Charles approved. "You can imagine how persuasive Rollo will be in the House of Lords. He is just the right person to head a Crusade of one kind or another."

"That is what I will make him do," Kyla said, "and I know he will be wonderful and win, just as he won today."

She looked up at the Earl adoringly.

He knew that she had given him the answer to the question he had asked himself when he had left Paris.

It was what did he want in life?

What he wanted, although he had not known it then, was somebody like Kyla, somebody he could love and somebody who at the same time would inspire him to do great deeds.

To bring happiness and security to the country just as he wanted to bring it to those he loved.

As it flashed through his mind, he knew how lucky he was.

As he looked at Kyla, he felt his love for her welling up inside him like a flood-tide.

It was a very different emotion from what he had ever felt before for any woman.

Then, as he went on looking at her, he realised that Charles had left the room and they were alone.

He put his arms round Kyla and drew her, almost roughly, close to him.

"I love you!" he said. "I love you so much that I feel a century will pass before you are my wife."

"You are really quite certain," she said a little hesitatingly, "that you are not – making a mistake?"

"I have never been so certain of anything ever," the Earl answered. "I know that we were made for each other. We are not two people but just one, my darling. Tonight I will explain to you exactly what that means."

Kyla moved a little closer to him.

"How can I have – been so – lucky?" she asked. "I prayed that we might – be saved and then God sent you to – save us."

"I believe that is true," the Earl said, "and that is why I want to tell you, my precious, that I will devote my whole life to making you happy and doing the things you want me to do and to be worthy of your love."

The way he spoke was very moving.

As Kyla felt the tears come into her eyes, he pulled her closer still.

She could hear angels singing songs of love and devotion.

Then, as he kissed her, she knew that he was carrying her into a Heaven that was all their own and that she would never have to run away again.

OTHER BOOKS IN THIS SERIES

The Barbara Cartland Eternal Collection is the unique opportunity to collect all five hundred of the timeless beautiful romantic novels written by the world's most celebrated and enduring romantic author.

Named the Eternal Collection because Barbara's inspiring stories of pure love, just the same as love itself, the books will be published on the internet at the rate of four titles per month until all five hundred are available.

The Eternal Collection, classic pure romance available worldwide for all time.

Made in the USA
Coppell, TX
10 September 2022

82919794R00114